BAYOU HEAT

ALEXANDRA IVY

LAURA WRIGHT

Copyright © 2016 by Alexandra Ivy & Laura Wright
All Rights Reserved.

Layout by www.formatting4U.com

No part of this work may be reproduced in any fashion without the express, written consent of the copyright holder.

Bayou Heat is a work of fiction. All characters and events portrayed herein are fictitious and are not based on any real persons living or dead.

ICE

ALEXANDRA IVY

PROLOGUE

Despite the chilly January weather, the Wildlands was thriving.

The home of the puma shifters, known as Pantera, was hidden deep in the swamps of Louisiana. Less than a year ago, the magical land had been tainted by a crazed goddess, nearly driving the Pantera to the edge of extinction. But now the lush vegetation had returned, as well as the Dyesse lily that was found only in the Wildlands and was filled with the magic of the land.

And even more astonishing, the Pantera were thriving. After fifty years of infertility, they now had nurseries that held a few precious cubs, with more on the way.

But not everything was perfect.

After secluding themselves from the world for decades, they'd discovered that an immoral, ruthless human had been kidnapping and using the Pantera in his hidden laboratories.

They'd managed to rescue several of their people who were tortured for years, as well as the human "lab rats" who were given large doses of Pantera blood and

DNA. They'd also succeeded in destroying several of the facilities owned by Benson Enterprises.

But their enemies were not about to concede defeat.

Not without a fight…

ICE
ALEXANDRA IVY

CHAPTER 1

Cammy Taylor hurried toward the sweeping colonial building with a wide, columned terrace and upper balcony. Painted white with black shutters, and topped by a steep roof, it had a distinct "Gone With The Wind" vibe.

Until the past few months it'd served as the headquarters for two of the Pantera factions. The Geeks, who were in charge of dealing with all technology. And the Diplomats, or Suits, as they were affectionately known. Now, however, the Hunters had started to use the building as well. It made it easier to coordinate the protection of the Wildlands as well as develop a strategy for tracking down their enemies.

Only the Nurturers still maintained their separate offices, in the nearby clinic.

Entering the large reception area, Cammy headed directly toward the conference room at the back. She was only distantly aware of the numerous males who halted in their tracks to watch her walk by. She was accustomed to the fascination with her long raven black hair that contrasted with the pure ivory of her skin, as well as her deep violet eyes that were rimmed with long black lashes. Her features were delicately carved and her body lush with feminine curves.

But it wasn't just her beauty that attracted attention.

It was the liquid grace of her movements, which marked her as a lethal Hunter, that seemed to stir the male Pantera's fantasies. As if the combination of soft femininity and predatory power was some sort of aphrodisiac.

Entering the room that held a long table in the center of the wood planked floor, and a bank of windows that overlooked the misty bayou, Cammy paused near the door. There were already a dozen Pantera seated at the table, filling the room with an electric tension, but her gaze instinctively sought out the male who was seated next to his mate.

Rage had been her best friend since they were both training to become Hunters. He was gorgeous, charming, and utterly loyal. And despite the fact that he'd bounced from one bed to another, she'd somehow convinced herself they would eventually settle down together.

Stupid, of course. Their cats had never been more than friends and casual lovers. Certainly her animal hadn't scented him as her mate. But her human side had weaved dreams of a future together. Dreams that had been destroyed the second she'd caught sight of him with the tiny female Geek when he'd returned to the Wildlands.

The two of them practically glowed with their love for one another.

Cammy clenched her teeth as pain lashed through her. Okay. She'd been an idiot. But that didn't make it easier to witness Rage totally besotted with his mate.

Feeling a watchful gaze, Cammy abruptly turned her head to catch sight of the Hunter standing in the corner. Ice Richelieu. A strange sensation tingled through her body as her gaze lingered on the stark beauty of his chiseled features and the shimmer of gold in the hair that brushed his broad, broad shoulders.

He was a fellow Hunter, but there was nothing about him that reminded her of Rage. He was older, for one thing. And for another, he'd moved around the world with his parents who were Diplomats. His foreign travels allowed him to be trained by a dozen different experts in various fighting styles.

Oh, and there was the indubitable fact that there was nothing charming about him. He was stoic, grim-faced, and inclined to hold himself aloof from his fellow Pantera.

Most unnerving of all, there was a savage hint of disdain in his icy blue eyes whenever he glanced in her direction. As if he found her unbearably obnoxious.

Pressing her lips together, she deliberately turned her back on the Hunter, her inner cat huffing in annoyance. Other females might ooh and ahh over his large, muscular body that looked as hard as granite beneath his black T-shirts and faded jeans. Or shiver at the hint of feral sensuality that promised all sorts of wicked pleasure.

But not Cammy. Truthfully, she did her best to avoid him.

Taking a seat at the end of the table, she thankfully turned her attention toward the two males who strolled into the room.

Raphael was the leader of the Suits. He was tall

and lean, with a golden beauty that was emphasized by his elegant suit. In contrast, Parish, the head of the Hunters, was dressed in jeans and a sweatshirt. He had long black hair, broad shoulders and his handsome face was marred with scars that bisected his cheek from his right ear down to his mouth. The two couldn't look more different, but they both possessed the thunderous power of alpha cats.

Instantly everyone in the room sat and stood a little straighter.

"Is everyone here?" Raphael demanded.

It was Rage's new mate who answered.

"Xavier wasn't able to come. He's still trying to decrypt the files from the computer we brought back from Bossier City," Lucie explained. Xavier was the leader of the Geeks and lately rarely left his offices upstairs, even to sleep. He was convinced there was vital intel in the data that could help them track down their enemies. "He said to send him an email."

Parish rolled his eyes. "Typical."

Raphael nodded, his eyes darkening with the power of his cat as he glanced around the room. "Let's get this started," he stated in grim tones. "We all know why we're here. Sadly, we've underestimated our enemy." Low growls rumbled through the room in agreement. "We originally thought they were nothing more than a small group of humans who could be hunted down and eliminated. Now we realize they're an international corporation with bottomless funds and friends in powerful positions. Worse, we now know they've been taking our people and creating serums out of our blood for longer than we ever imagined."

Raphael's face tightened with the frustration they all felt. "Which means we have to get our asses in gear and play catch-up."

Ice spoke from the corner. "Do we have any hard targets?"

"Not yet," Raphael admitted. They'd managed to discover a few "clinics" and burn them to the ground. Frustratingly, however, there were still more out there. And worse, the enemy's leader continued to elude them. "But we have the Healers working with those who were held in the various labs. We're hoping they can remember something that will lead us to Christopher."

Parish's eyes glowed with the golden power of his puma. "Then it's our turn for games."

There was a short pause as they all savored the day the Pantera would destroy their enemies once and for all.

Finally Cammy asked the obvious question. "What do you want from us?"

It was Raphael who answered. "Until we can go on the attack I want to make certain the bastards don't get their hands on any more of our people. I've called back all Pantera to the Wildlands."

Cammy nodded. The leader of the Diplomats didn't need to say that there would be Pantera spies still out looking for the bad guys. They all knew this temporary retreat didn't mean surrender. More an opportunity to regroup so they could strike even harder the next time.

"The guard patrols will be doubled," Parish said. "I don't want anyone scouting the perimeter alone."

"What about the new pack members?" Ice demanded.

The new pack members included the Pantera they'd discovered in the various Benson laboratories, as well as the human "rats" and "brood mares" who'd been used and abused by their captors.

Over the past weeks they'd been building several new cottages, as well as a small community center for them along the edge of Wildlands. It allowed them to travel in and out of their section without worrying about the Wildlands' magical barrier that kept out most humans.

"What about them?" Raphael asked.

"Shouldn't they be moved deeper into the interior?" Ice demanded, his voice low and laced with an authority that revealed the dominance of his cat. "They're dangerously exposed."

"I agree." Raphael grimaced. "Unfortunately the humans, and even a few of the hybrids, are still not entirely comfortable at the thought of being behind our magical shields where they can't move in and out without help from a Pantera. They spent too much time locked behind bars to accept we're not trying to put them back in a prison."

Ice nodded his head, his chiseled features impossible to read. "Understandable, but they need to consider the safety of their children."

Raphael nodded. He was a fierce leader, but he was always willing to listen to the suggestions of his trusted advisors, whether they were Suits or Hunters or Nurturers.

"I'll speak with them again," he promised.

"Maybe we should think about having a public meeting where they can express their concerns, and we can do our best to meet their needs. If they're to become a part of our clan they need to have a voice in their future."

Cammy smiled with wry admiration. Raphael's skill as a Diplomat would be as important to their future as Parish's skill as a warrior.

The conversation turned to the rotation of guards, as well as starting a training program for the Pantera who'd been held by their enemies. Cammy, however, found her attention drifting toward the male in the corner.

It wasn't the first time her gaze strayed in Ice's direction. Or lingered on the compelling beauty of his face. She told herself it was out of self-defense. How could she avoid him if she didn't know where he was?

It didn't explain why her attention lingered…but hey, who cared?

She was still watching him when he abruptly tensed, his gaze locked on something outside the window.

"Intruder," he snarled, his low voice attracting the attention of everyone in the room.

"Where?" Parish demanded, moving with liquid speed to stand at Ice's side.

Ice pointed. "There."

There was a rush of movement as the various Pantera hurried to get a glimpse of who had captured Ice's attention. Cammy was short enough that she had to wiggle through the bodies pressed tightly together before she could finally catch sight of the man who was running at top speed toward the building.

Cammy frowned. He wasn't Pantera, although he was moving with more grace than any mere human. A hybrid? There were a few who had enough Pantera in their blood to pass easily through the magical shield.

"I'll deal with him," Parish snapped, stepping back as he prepared to unleash his puma.

Raphael grabbed his arm before he could shift. "Wait, Parish," he warned, nodding toward the intruder. "Look."

At that moment the stiff January breeze tugged open the man's jacket. They all gasped in horror. Strapped to the intruder's slender body was a series of long, narrow tubes held together by narrow wires.

"Suicide bomber," Parish ground out in disbelief, reaching for the handgun holstered at his lower back. "Hit the alarm," he snapped toward Rage before turning his attention to Ice. "Get the building evacuated."

Parish shoved up the window and opened fire. The man faltered but continued forward, his dark hair tousled and his eyes wild. Cammy was turning away when an explosion rocked the ground beneath her feet.

Crap.

Obviously realizing he wasn't going to make it inside the building, the suicide bomber must have set off his charges. And while he hadn't managed to do the damage he no doubt wanted, the explosion was large enough to blast a massive hole in the wall, collapsing the back of the building.

Cammy darted toward the doorway even as the upper floor came crashing down, threatening to crush them. The sound of furious snarls and the piercing shrill of the siren deafened her, making it impossible to hear the shout of warning as a heavy beam fell directly toward her head.

One moment she was urging the last of her friends through the doorway, and the next she was flat on her back with Ice perched on top of her. She went rigid with shock. What the hell was he doing?

Then she heard the beam hit the floor only inches from her head with shattering force. *Holy shit.* If Ice hadn't shoved her out of the way…

She glanced up at the hard face, her breath snaring in her throat at the ice blue eyes that studied her with an emotion she couldn't decipher.

Without warning, her cat restlessly stirred beneath her skin. Almost as if it wanted to rub against Ice, and coat itself in his raw, male scent.

Good…Goddess.

Thankfully unaware of her baffling reaction to the feel of his large form pressing her against the floor, Ice was rolling upward and tugging her to her feet.

"Are you okay?" he demanded, his tone clipped.

"Yeah, I'm fine." She glanced around the shattered room that now looked like a war zone. "What the hell was that?"

Ice's expression was grim as he reached to grab her hand, tugging her out of the room.

"First we make sure everyone is safe. Then we'll figure out who attacked us," he growled. "And how we intend to punish them."

***

Ice was stronger, faster, and more ruthless than most Pantera. Which was what made him such a good Hunter. But after hours of searching through every inch of the Wildlands to make certain there were no enemies lurking in the gathering dusk, he was exhausted.

Still he forced himself to make another sweep to search for any wounded Pantera before he at last headed toward the communal area where the majority of his people were gathered. His gaze instinctively sought out his parents who'd returned home the previous week. They were with his grandmother as she moved among the wounded, using her Healer gifts on the handful of injured people. Next, his gaze skimmed toward Cammy as she stood guard over a group of young who were huddled in the center of the clearing.

At a distance she looked as weary as he felt, but she was standing with her spine straight and her head high. Which assured him she wasn't injured.

A tightness he didn't even realize was wrapped around his chest slowly eased.

He didn't know when his cat had decided Cammy was his to protect. It'd come on so slowly he hadn't recognized the danger until it was too late. Now he simply accepted that his cat wasn't going to change its stubborn mind.

Even if she was obsessed with Rage.

Shaking his head, he veered around the edge of the mossy area. He had returned to report to Parish. Once he finished speaking with his leader he was going to grab some food and head back out to do another search of the outer perimeter.

It didn't matter how tired he was. There would be no sleep for any of them tonight.

At last finding his leader near the badly damaged Headquarters, Ice waited for Parish to finish his conversation with Raphael and Xavier. Five minutes later Parish was moving to stand directly in front of him, his expression grim.

"You finished your sweep?"

"Yeah. They're gone," Ice assured him. "I count at least a half dozen entered, although it was impossible to determine if they all left."

"You checked the caves?"

Ice nodded. The magic of the Wildlands included several deep caverns, despite the swampy landscape.

"I searched them," Ice said. "And then I returned to search them again before heading back here in case they doubled back."

"How many entry points?"

"One on the northern edge."

"That matches with Keira," Parish said, referring to his sister who was one of the best Hunters in the Wildlands.

Ice glanced toward the Headquarters, which was leaning at a drunken angle and still smoldering. "What's the damage here?"

Parish folded his arms over his chest, his jaw clenched. "It's going to have to be bulldozed and rebuilt, but that's not the worst part. Xavier's equipment was trashed when the floor collapsed. Plus we had to use water to put out the fire that was started by the explosion."

Ice grimaced. Fire and water wasn't a good

combo for electronics. "What about the computers that belonged to Benson Enterprises?"

"Destroyed."

Ice's breath hissed through his teeth. Fury scoured through him like lava, but he was doing his best to keep his emotions leashed. He'd learned from his sensei that anger was the enemy.

Only a clear mind could reveal a pathway to success.

"Damn," he muttered.

"Xavier has everything stored on a remote server," Parish continued, "but it's going to take time to get him back up and running."

Knowing there was nothing he could do to help the Geeks, Ice turned his attention to the Pantera who were huddled in groups in the center of the large clearing. "What about casualties?" he asked.

"Several injured, but no one dead, thank the Goddess," Parish responded. "And thanks to you. If you hadn't spotted the intruder who knows what might have happened."

Ice waved aside his leader's words. He was lucky to be standing where he'd had a clear view of the trail leading out of the bogs. "Did you check with our newest pack members?" he asked, referring to those living on the edge of the Wildlands.

"They didn't sense any intruders in their area," Parish answered.

"Good."

Parish nodded, although they both knew it'd been sheer luck that none of the outer cabins had been attacked. "They'll be moved into temporary housing until we can be sure it's safe for them to return."

A sensible precaution.

"Do we know how he got through the shield?" Ice demanded.

"We're assuming he had enough Pantera blood to slip through the magic," Parish said. The barrier was intended to protect the puma shifters from the outside world, but it wasn't a foolproof form of security. As they were painfully discovering. "We don't know if he was injected with or blood or altered with DNA to become a hybrid."

Ice grimaced, assuming the Healers would use the bits and pieces left of the intruder to determine if he was a born Pantera, or if he'd been injected with their blood. "It was a risky play," he said. "They couldn't know we would be meeting at that precise time. Not unless there's a spy in the Wildlands."

Parish shrugged. "The Headquarters might not have been the target. Suicide bombers usually go for maximum carnage. He could have been headed for the communal center, hoping we were gathered for dinner, or even the clinic where we keep our most vulnerable. But after he was shot he might have been forced to blow up the nearest object before he bled out."

Ice frowned, slowly replaying the incident in his mind. The man had run out of the thick vegetation of the wetlands, seeming to head straight toward them. But the pathway circled the Headquarters and ended at the communal center. That could easily have been his destination.

"But why strike at all?" he murmured, asking the question that had been preying on his mind while he was searching for intruders.

Parish frowned, as if he hadn't had time to consider what had prompted the attack. "We've done damage to them. I'm sure they want some revenge."

"Maybe."

Parish easily sensed Ice's hesitation. "What are you thinking?"

Ice struggled to pinpoint his vague sense they were missing something.

Something important.

"It could be a lone nut job wanting revenge," he slowly murmured.

"Or?" Parish prompted when Ice hesitated.

"Or a distraction," Ice at last said.

Parish's eyes abruptly narrowed. "You're right. We need to prepare…" The words trailed away as Parish glanced toward the crowd of shell-shocked Pantera. "Shit." He gave a frustrated shake of his head. "I don't even know what we need to prepare for."

Ice grimaced. What could he say? None of them knew what might be coming next.

They stood in mutual silence, both lost in their dark thoughts when Indy came to a skidding halt next to Parish.

The tiny female with short, midnight black hair and dark blue eyes looked like a biker pixie doll. She was one of the lab rats who'd escaped from the Benson labs and had been conducting a vigilante war against the humans when Angel found her.

"I need your help," she bluntly commanded.

Indy had the same social skills as Ice.

Precisely none.

Parish instantly turned to face her. "Tell me."

"Karen is missing."

Ice frowned. It took him a minute to recall the pretty woman who'd been with Indy when the Pantera had found the rats in New Orleans. She'd been a brood mare for the humans, which meant she'd been inseminated, by force, with Pantera semen to produce hybrids. She had one son, Caleb, with her in the Wildlands, but Ice seemed to recall that he'd heard she had other children who had been taken from her at birth.

"Where is she supposed to be?" Parish demanded.

"She was at the clinic when the explosion went off," Indy said. "No one remembers seeing her after that."

Parish frowned. "Could she have gone home?"

Indy looked at him in disbelief. "No way in hell. If there were injuries, she wouldn't have left the clinic even if she was ready to collapse."

"Take me to the last place she was seen," Parish ordered Indy before he was glancing over his shoulder at Ice. "Come with me."

Ice instantly fell into step with Parish as Indy headed toward the long building that was bustling with activity.

"She has an office in the clinic," Indy told them, leading them toward the nearest door.

On a normal day, the healing center was a place of peace, with cherry-paneled walls and hand-woven rugs that had little semblance to a human hospital. Tonight, however, the peace had been replaced with a sizzling energy as the Healers worked together to cure the wounded and soothe those traumatized by the attack.

Avoiding the treatment rooms, Indy moved

toward the long corridor where there was a line of offices. She opened the door at the end, and instantly Ice's cat went Hunter-still.

A swift glance revealed a broken window, and files scattered over the floor. There'd been a recent struggle. But that wasn't what had his puma pressing beneath his skin.

It was the unmistakable scent that filled the air.

"Blood," he breathed. "And the musk of an unfamiliar Pantera."

Indy made a sound of distress, her hand pressed to her chest as Parish went to his knees to study the stain in the center of the rug. "Is she…?"

"She was alive when she left here," Parish reassured the young female, straightening to make a quick sweep of the small room.

There wasn't much to see. A desk with a computer, two chairs, and floor-to-ceiling shelves that were stuffed with file folders.

"I know she worked with the Healers. Was she doing anything else?" Parish asked, clearly leaping to the assumption that the enemy had taken the woman.

Not that it was much of a leap.

What else could have happened?

Indy visibly squared her shoulders, putting aside her fear so she could do whatever necessary to help her friend. "What do you mean?"

Parish nodded his head toward the files. "Was she doing any research?"

Indy chewed her bottom lip. "I know she was still trying to locate her sons. Xavier was working with her. He downloaded and printed out the patient files from the various Benson Enterprise computers we've gotten our hands on."

"I meant any research that involves your people," Parish explained.

"*Our* people," Indy corrected him.

It took a minute for Parish to realize she was insisting the refugees were now a part of the Pantera pack.

"Yes. *Our* people," he agreed, his tone impatient.

Satisfied, Indy wrapped her arms around her waist, her face pale. "She was working with Doc Chelsea. They were testing her blood to see what Benson Enterprises did to alter her."

"I know she was a brood mare—" Parish bit off his words with a grimace. "Sorry."

"It's okay," Indy assured him. "It was a term Karen used. She said there was no point in running from what had been done to us. We had to accept it and use the pain to make our future better."

Ice remained silent, even as he inwardly applauded the woman's philosophy. Most people who'd endured what she had would be too bitter to embrace life to the fullest.

"Did they discover what was done to her?" Parish asked.

Indy shrugged. "As far as I know they were still working on the results."

Parish planted his fists on his hips, staring at the window. "Maybe someone didn't want us finding out the exact nature of the experiments."

Ice wasn't convinced. "How could they know she was being tested?"

"Karen had a friend who she kept in contact with in New York," Indy offered. "She might have said something that could have been passed on to Christopher and his band of bastards."

"So it's possible the bomber could have been a distraction to get their hands on Karen," Parish murmured in preoccupied tones. He glanced toward Ice. "See if you can find a trail."

With a nod, Ice headed across the office, carefully climbing out the broken window. Once on the mossy ground, he drew in a deep breath, locking on the scent of the unknown Pantera. Karen's scent would be throughout the Wildlands. It would be easier to follow the smell of the intruder.

Focused on his goal, he blocked out the curious gazes that followed him as he circled past the far edge of the destroyed Headquarters and down a side path that was rarely used. It headed through the deepest part of the bogs and the ground was too soft to build homes on.

Coming to a halt, Ice closed his eyes, emptying his mind as he called on the power of his puma. Tingles of magic vibrated through him, lengthening muscle and sinew and popping bones into place. Then in a final burst of heat, he was fully shifted.

With a roar of pleasure, his cat leaped forward, easily moving over the soggy ground. He was swiftly following the trail, not surprised to find one set of footprints. Karen had no doubt been knocked out to keep her quiet as they took her from her office. They would have to carry her out of the Wildlands.

Unless…no. He would smell her blood if they'd killed her and dumped her body in the bogs.

Jumping over the fallen tree trunks and narrow channels, Ice finally reached the edge of the Wildlands.

Whoever had taken Karen had met up with the other intruders, and they'd all left at the same spot he'd discovered earlier. Remaining within the magic of the Wildlands so he could stay in his cat form, he followed the edge of the road that skirted the bayous, heading toward La Pierre, a small town just a few miles away.

Hoping he could capture them before they managed to escape, Ice growled with frustration when the scent abruptly disappeared. He didn't need the deep ruts in the muddy ground to tell him that a car had been waiting for them.

Unable to follow them, Ice headed back into the Wildlands, finding Parish waiting for him outside the clinic.

With a burst of magic he shifted, shivering at the agonizing pleasure of transforming back so quickly. "They took off in a vehicle that must have been waiting for them."

Indy stepped out of the shadows. "We have to get her back."

"We will," Parish said, his gaze never leaving Ice. "Is it possible to track them?"

"No." Ice shook his head. He was a hell of a Hunter, but he wasn't a miracle worker. "They must have left just after the explosion. There's no way to know which direction they went once they hit the paved road."

Parish paused, his gaze skimming over the gathered Pantera as if seeking inspiration. Then, with a quicksilver movement, he was turning toward Indy. "Do you have anything of Karen's that holds a deep emotional attachment for her?"

"Yes," she said without hesitation. "I'll be right back."

Ice narrowed his gaze, a sharp-edged suspicion twisting his gut in a knot. "Parish—"

"We need to get her back," Parish interrupted.

"Right now we need to concentrate on making sure the Wildlands are safe," Ice growled.

Parish took a step closer, his voice pitched low enough it wouldn't carry. It was easier to sprout wings and fly than to have a private conversation in the middle of a pack of shifters.

"If the enemy went to this much trouble to get their hands on Karen, she must have something that either is vital or possesses a danger to them. Which means she's an asset to us we can't afford to lose," Parish said, his tone bleak. Was he blaming himself for the enemy slipping past their borders? "Besides, she has too much sensitive information on our people to leave her in their hands."

Before Ice could speak, the young female was returning, handing Parish a small picture of an unknown woman in a golden frame.

"Here," she said. "This is Karen's mother. She died before Karen managed to escape. It's all she has left of her."

Parish gave the picture to Ice. "Take this to Cammy. See if she can use her powers to find Karen."

Ice paused. It wasn't that he didn't believe in Cammy's ability to track down Karen. He didn't understand her strange talent for using objects to find people, but he knew that it was very real.

No. His hesitation came from his ingrained habit of trying to avoid the young Hunter. That part of him urged him to ask Parish to send another Hunter with Cammy. The leader wouldn't be happy, but he would accept Ice's demand to remain and help guard the Wildlands.

It's what he would've done just a few days ago.

But everything had changed when Rage returned home with a mate.

Now…

"Fine," he muttered, his gaze seeking out the female who'd fascinated and aggravated him for years.

Parish laid a hand on his shoulder. "Stay in touch."

CHAPTER 2

Cammy jogged to the edge of the Wildlands, carrying the backpack that she'd hastily stuffed with a change of clothes, a few toiletries and her favorite gun. She was dressed in leather pants and a black turtleneck sweater and heavy boots, with her hair pulled into a tight braid.

Her entire body tingled. She told herself it was a combination of delayed shock and eagerness to strike back at their enemies.

It couldn't have anything to do with spending the next few hours alone with Ice. Could it?

Okay, there'd been a moment when he'd rescued her from the falling beam. Heat and heart-thumping awareness. And she couldn't completely ignore the fact that her cat roared with anticipation when Ice had sought her out to tell her that they were going on the hunt for the missing Karen.

But still...

Her tangled thoughts were interrupted as she caught the rich scent of Ice's musk. The tingling intensified, sending a strange quiver down her spine as he stepped from the shadows of the cypress tree.

His large body was emphasized by the tight black

T-shirt he was wearing despite the sharp chill in the air, and the worn jeans that clung to his narrow backside and muscular thighs.

A part of her had always known he was a stunning creature. The male features that looked as if they'd been sculpted by the hands of an artist. The golden hair that brushed his wide shoulders. And the pale, pale eyes that glowed with the power of his cat.

But until this moment, she'd never allowed herself to savor the full impact of his savage beauty.

Dear Goddess, what was happening to her? She never felt all shivery when she was with Rage. Or any other male. So what was up with Ice?

Thankfully unaware of her weird reaction to his presence, Ice moved to stand at her side.

"You ready?" he demanded, smart enough not to suggest he take her bag. She appreciated good manners, but she was a Hunter. She could carry her own damned equipment.

"Yeah." She headed toward the Jeep parked just down the road. "The sooner we do this, the sooner we can get back."

With long strides, he was quickly walking at her side. "In a hurry?" he taunted in soft tones.

She glanced over her shoulder, her features softening as she recalled her last sight of Rage as he'd been standing guard over those Pantera who were sleeping in the communal center.

"We're needed in the Wildlands," she murmured.

She heard a low growl rumble in Ice's chest. "You're needed with me," he snapped. "*He's* with the person he needs at his side."

Cammy flinched. Had he known she was thinking about Rage?

The suspicion was enough to stiffen her spine with humiliation.

"I don't know what you're talking about," she said between gritted teeth, wrenching open the door of the vehicle and climbing into the passenger seat.

Only an idiot would think that Ice would let her drive.

A few seconds later Ice was settled behind the steering wheel, his hand reaching to start the engine. But instead of putting the vehicle in gear, he instead turned to study her with an unnerving intensity.

"Look, we're going to have to work together, Cammy," he said, his husky voice stroking over her like a caress. "Can you do that?"

Could she? In the enclosed space of the Jeep she could feel the zap of his intense energy racing over her skin. It was like standing in the center of an electric storm. And worse, her cat was continuing to try and reach out. As if it was longing to touch Ice's animal.

It was only her stubborn pride that refused to admit she might be in over her head.

"I can if you can," she found herself saying.

A slow, terrifyingly smug smile curved his lips.

"Which way?" he asked.

With an effort, Cammy forced herself to concentrate on the framed picture she held in her hands. She'd worry about Ice and her aggravating response to him later. For now, nothing mattered but tracking down Karen.

"North," she murmured, focusing on the familiar sensation that tugged at her.

Without question, Ice put the vehicle in gear and turned onto the first road that headed north.

The thick darkness cloaked around them, but Ice didn't turn on the headlights. Their cat eyes ensured they could see as well at night as during the day, and there was no point in attracting unwanted attention.

They traveled in silence, the Jeep churning through the muddy potholes. It wasn't until they'd reached the paved road that led out of the wetlands that Ice glanced toward her with blatant curiosity. "How does your power work?"

Cammy didn't mind the question. She'd never met another Pantera who had her unique gift, so it was understandable that someone who was working with her would want to know what to expect.

She far preferred that they just ask than to speculate behind her back.

"When I touch an object that's emotionally connected to a person, I can sense where they are," she said.

He returned his gaze to the road. "That's it?"

"That's it."

"Is it magic?"

Cammy shrugged. During her childhood there had been a rigorous effort to figure out where her gift came from. Now she refused any more testing. It didn't matter where it came from, just that it worked when she needed it.

"No one really knows. I've been tested by the Healers, and even the elders, but no one has figured out the how or why," she said.

He accepted the lack of explanation with a nod.

"How close do you have to be to the person you're searching for?"

"The farther they are away, the less accuracy I have," she admitted. "I can tell the general direction, like a compass, but no specific address. As I get nearer I can start to pinpoint an exact location."

He picked up speed as the road widened. "How did you discover your talent?"

Her lips twitched at the memory. "I was in nursery school when one of my friends went missing. We were sent to our homes so the pack could gather together and start a search. I grabbed the missing cub's favorite ball so I could give it to him when he was found." She gave a low chuckle. While the pack had been in a frantic search, she'd merrily led her mother straight to the caves that were a favorite playground for the young cubs. "As soon as I touched it I knew he was hiding in one of the caves to play a trick on our teacher."

The air was abruptly scented with the musk of Ice's cat. Cammy's nose twitched. She could smell his sudden surge of anger.

"Let me guess—the cub was Rage," he snarled.

Cammy frowned, studying the stark lines of his profile. "Why does Rage bother you?"

"He doesn't," he growled. Then, with a visible effort, he eased his clenched muscles. "Not anymore."

Cammy blinked. "What's that mean?"

"Exactly what I said." He lifted one shoulder. "I no longer need to concern myself with Rage."

Cammy shook her head. Ice had never truly fit in with her and her friends.

When he'd decided to remain in the Wildlands rather than continue to travel with his parents, he'd instantly been elevated to the upper ranks of the Hunters. Not surprising with his skills, but it hadn't sat well with all the younger males. And his lack of interest in trying to become a part of their group had only deepened the resentment.

"Always so cryptic," she muttered.

He shrugged. "I've never seen the point in using a hundred words when I can use ten."

"Yeah, right," she muttered. "You just like playing the role of the mystical, always-aloof Ice."

There was an unexpected silence, and Cammy realized she'd struck a nerve. It was obvious in the tight line of his jaw and his white-knuckled clench on the steering wheel.

"I wasn't raised in the Wildlands," he said in low tones. "I didn't develop the same bond with our packmates that you find so easy."

Regret flared through her. Ice had always been so...reserved, she'd never considered the fact that he might not be comfortable in their company. Now she was forced to accept that she hadn't been fair. She'd blamed her own unease in his presence on him.

"It must have been lonely," she murmured.

He shot her a startled glance, clearly unprepared for her attempt to offer an olive branch.

"At times," he admitted. "But I had schooling from top scholars around the world and the ability to develop a variety of fighting skills. And, of course, we returned to the Wildlands every few months to release our cats."

A part of her envied his travels. Her own parents

rarely left the Wildlands, considering humans as dangerous beasts who should be avoided at all costs. Which meant that Cammy had a very limited opportunity to discover the world.

"Why didn't you join us when you decided to return home?" she demanded.

He returned his gaze to the road. Was there something he was hiding from her?

"I was more advanced," he said. "It made more sense to spend my time with the mature Pantera."

She rolled her eyes. Okay. She wasn't entirely to blame for their awkward relationship.

"Arrogant ass," she muttered.

His lips twitched. "Possibly."

"Definitely."

Ice was smart enough not to argue. He *was* an arrogant ass. Although Cammy was beginning to suspect it wasn't so much conceit as it was sheer confidence, combined with an introverted nature.

They drove several miles before Ice abruptly broke the silence.

"I've explained my occasional discomfort in being a part of the gang," he said.

Cammy arched a brow. "Gang?"

He ignored her taunting. "Now it's your turn. Why do you go to such efforts to avoid me?"

"I don't—" She bit off her instinctive denial as he shot her a narrow-eyed glare. Could he read her mind? "Okay. I might avoid you."

"Why?"

She hunched her shoulders. "I see how you look at me."

He jerked, as if she'd struck him. "How do I look at you?"

She glared at him. Did he think she was stupid? Not even a blind female could have been unaware of his lingering gaze.

"Like I'm a bug who just crawled from beneath a rock," she snapped.

The Jeep abruptly slowed as he took his foot off the gas pedal, gazing at her in pure disbelief. "That's what you think?"

She gave a slow nod, caught off guard when he tilted back his head to laugh with shocking amusement.

Cammy scowled, angered by his reaction even as her heart missed a beat. *Heavens.* He was always gorgeous. But when he laughed his features lost their stark edges and his eyes became a luminous blue.

"I don't know what's so funny," she muttered.

His gaze swept over her flushed face, lingering on the soft curve of her lips before he returned his attention to the road. "Trust me. I've never once thought of you as a bug."

Feeling oddly vulnerable, Cammy glanced toward the twinkle of lights that indicated a town not far ahead.

"I doubt you've ever thought about me at all," she said.

"Which just proves how little you know me."

Cammy pressed her lips together. She didn't understand this male. Rage had been charming and open and utterly uncomplicated.

But Ice...

He was like an intricate puzzle that fascinated her at the same time as he completely frustrated her.

Giving a shake of her head, Cammy concentrated on the tiny tug that warned her they needed to make a turn.

"We need to veer to the east," she said.

"Damn," Ice muttered.

"What's wrong?"

"They must be headed for the interstate," he said, his tone threaded with resignation. "I was hoping they would stop at a nearby house."

Cammy grimaced. "Since when have our enemies ever made anything easy?"

"True."

Settling back in his seat, Ice took the exit that would lead them to the interstate as the dawn crested the horizon to paint the sky with gentle shades of pink.

***

Karen woke from her deep sleep to discover she was currently locked in a cage with heavy steel bars.

Gasping in shock, she rolled to the side, tumbling off the narrow cot she was lying on, directly onto a hard cement floor. She groaned as the impact sent a bolt of pain through her aching head. What the heck? Lying on her side, she took in the long room that was brightly lit from the fluorescent lights in the ceiling. There were industrial cabinets lining one wall and stainless steel walk-in refrigerators that lined another. In the center of the room was a gurney that was surrounded by rolling trays that were usually found in hospitals.

This was a laboratory. And she was locked in a cage.

Just like the one she'd been trapped in for over twelve years.

Her stomach cramped, fear momentarily paralyzing her. Then, with a fierce effort, she called on the courage that had allowed her to survive.

No. Oh no. Not again.

She'd been a victim once, but she'd be damned if she was ever going to be a victim again.

Gritting her teeth, Karen managed to force herself to her hands and knees, crawling toward the door of her cramped prison. She'd just managed to wrap her hands around the bars when she heard the unmistakable sound of approaching footsteps.

"Hello?" she called out. "Is anyone there?"

"Good," a low male voice spoke from the shadows of a door on the far side of the lab. "You're awake."

She froze. There was something familiar about that voice. It scratched at the edge of her mind.

Was it one of her previous abusers?

"Who's there?"

There was a small pause. "It's not the time for introductions," the mystery man at last drawled. "Not yet."

"At least step into the light so I can see you."

"I don't think so."

Karen frowned. Why would he hide?

"Can you at least tell me where I am?"

"Someplace where you'll be safe."

"Is that a joke?" Karen's fingers tightened on the

bars, giving the door a shake. Not surprisingly it wouldn't budge. "I'm locked in a cage like an animal. That doesn't feel safe to me."

"A necessary precaution," the stranger murmured, almost as if he was trying to soothe her.

Karen blinked back tears. She'd been working in her office in the Pantera Wildlands when she'd heard the explosion, swiftly followed by the sound of her window being busted in. She'd had less than a split second to catch sight of an intruder dressed in black entering the room before she felt a fist connecting with her mouth, swiftly followed by another punch to her temple.

After that everything had gone dark.

"I don't understand," she breathed. "Why was I taken?"

The man clicked his tongue. As if he was growing impatient with her questions. "I told you. To keep you safe."

Karen refused to be silent. She was desperate to know what'd happened. "What about the others?"

"What others?"

"My friends. My—" She bit off her words. She didn't know why she'd been taken, which meant she didn't know whether or not to share the information that she had three biological sons. Two had already been stolen from her. The last thing she wanted was to make the only child she'd managed to save a target. But then again, if they'd known exactly where to find her, it was doubtful they didn't know about Caleb. "My son," she finished.

There was an unmistakable sound of disgust. "Their fates aren't my concern."

She tilted her chin to a defiant angle. "They are mine."

"In time you'll forget them," the unknown man drawled.

Her breath hissed through her teeth. The man was out of his mind if he thought she would ever forget her friends, let alone her sons.

"No," she hissed, her eyes narrowed. "Never."

A creepy laugh echoed through the lab. "You will. I know you better than you know yourself." There was a long pause before he at last whispered her name. "Karen."

Karen shuddered. *God almighty.*

This was different from the first time she'd been kidnapped.

Then, it'd been clinical. Brutally detached. She was a brood mare who was there to produce hybrid Pantera babies.

Now it felt oddly intimate. As if her capturer believed he actually knew her.

Which was more disturbing than being treated as a brood mare.

She might, however, be able to use his weird behavior to her advantage.

"Please, let me go," she pleaded in soft tones.

"Relax," he murmured. "I'll have dinner sent to you. I think you'll appreciate my chef. He once worked at a five-star hotel. Now he's pleased to serve me." His low chuckle sent a chill down her spine. "Just as you will."

She heard a shuffle, as if the stranger was turning to leave. Panic thundered through her. "Wait."

"I'll return when you've grown more accustomed to your new home," he promised.

The sound of retreating footsteps warned her that the brief encounter was at an end. She was alone.

Again.

With a low cry of despair, Karen leaned her head against the cold bars of her cell. "No."

CHAPTER 3

Ice exited the interstate, pulling to a halt in a rest area and putting the car into park.

For the past half hour Cammy had grown progressively more withdrawn, her brow creased with concern. Clearly there was something on her mind.

Turning in his seat, he studied her tense features. "Will you tell me what's wrong?"

She glanced out the window, her gaze sweeping over the pine trees that were bathed in gold in the early morning sunlight.

"I can sense Karen, but she feels very distant," she said. "More distant than she should be."

Ice frowned, not certain what she was trying to tell him. "We're not gaining on them?"

"No." She gave a decisive shake of her head. "I thought at first it was just because they had a head start on us. But..."

Her words trailed away, as if she was lost in her thoughts.

"Cammy?" he at last prompted.

"She's too far away for them to have driven," she at last said.

He considered a long moment, debating the various reasons that would explain Cammy's sense of distance.

It was possible that Karen had left the Wildlands before the explosion. No—Indy had indicated that Karen had been seen in the clinic not long before all hell had broken loose.

Which meant there was only one reasonable explanation.

"You think they flew?"

She gave a slow nod. "It would explain why we aren't gaining on them."

Ice parted his lips, only to snap them shut as he was struck by a sudden memory.

Putting the Jeep in gear, he was heading out of the rest area, taking the narrow access road rather than returning to the interstate.

"Hold on," he muttered as they jolted over the decaying pavement.

Cammy sent him a confused glance. "Where are we going?"

"The bastards who held Keira prisoner left the area using a private airfield not far from here," he said, referring to Parish's sister who'd been held prisoner by the humans. "I think we should check to see if we can find someone to question."

Cammy nodded her approval at his suggestion, sending a surge of warmth through Ice. He'd tried to deny his need for this female's respect, but it'd always been there, lurking just below the surface.

Doubling back, Ice took the rarely used roads that would lead to the airfield they'd discovered after Keira had been rescued. At the time, he and the other Hunters had been chasing the disciples who worshipped an evil goddess, Shakpi. Recently, however, they'd been searching for a direct connection to Benson Enterprises.

Less than ten minutes later he had the Jeep parked in a small copse of trees just off the road. It was the perfect location to study the large metal hangar with a bi-fold door that was built in the middle of the empty field. In front of the hangar was a cement pad that led to a grassy area that had been precisely trimmed to create a runway.

A quick glance assured them they were out of view, and rolling down the window he sniffed the air, able to sense there was only one human inside the hangar.

Perfect.

Cammy had her own window rolled down, breathing deeply of the morning air. "Karen was here."

"Yeah. I'm going to talk with the man inside." Ice reached into the backseat and grabbed a gray hoodie before he was sliding out of the Jeep. He waited for Cammy to join him as he pulled on the sweatshirt. "Stay here and keep watch," he commanded. "I prefer not to be interrupted."

She held up the handgun she'd obviously pulled out of her backpack. "No problem."

He resisted the urge to lean down and brush his mouth over the temptation of her lips. If he started kissing her, he was fairly certain he wasn't going to be able to stop.

Plus…she was holding a loaded gun.

Never a good combination when he wasn't sure if she wanted to be kissed.

Turning, he jogged toward the metal building, pulling up his hood to hide his face from any security cameras. He reached the side entrance and turned the knob. Locked. Tightening his grip, he slammed his shoulder against the metal door. It popped open and Ice stepped inside, swiftly searching the open space for the human.

There was the echo of footsteps coming from the back of the hangar, where a small prop plane was parked. Rounding the wing of the aircraft, a short, thickly muscled human with a buzzed haircut headed straight for Ice. His square face was flushed with anger as he barreled forward, clearly itching for a fight.

"Hey idiot, can't you read?" he barked. "This is private property."

Ice folded his arms over his chest. If his prey wanted to come to him, that was fine. It saved him the trouble of having to chase him.

"I'm looking for some friends of mine who used this airfield," he said. "I need to know when they left and where they went."

Unaware he was walking straight into a trap, the man continued forward. "Fuck off."

"That's not very nice."

Just steps away from Ice, the man reached for the gun that he had hidden beneath his leather jacket.

"Get out of here before I blow your brains—"

Ice's arm shot out as he wrapped his fingers around the man's thick neck. Then, with a brutal strength, he was lifting the stranger off his feet.

"Clearly your mother didn't teach you any manners," he murmured in smooth tones.

The man squirmed, his face turning an ugly shade of puce. "You don't know who you're screwing with. You hurt me and you're a dead man."

Ice gave a shake of his head, allowing his hood to fall back. "Do I look scared?"

The man gave a choked sound of shock as he caught sight of the glow in Ice's eyes. As if his ability to lift a grown-ass man off the ground with one hand hadn't revealed he was more than human.

Idiot.

"Shit," the man spit out. "You're one of those animals."

"Surprise." A humorless smile stretched Ice's lips. "Now answer my questions."

"I just got here an hour ago—"

The man's words broke off with an agonized gasp as Ice tightened his fingers, cutting off his air.

"Do you think I won't snap your neck?"

Dropping the gun, the man reached up to clutch at Ice's wrist, futilely trying to free himself.

"No. Please," he rasped, genuine fear flashing through his dark eyes. "I'll tell you."

Ice eased his grip, but he kept the man dangling off the ground. A little reminder that Ice could crush his throat if he wasn't happy with the man's answers.

"Talk," he commanded.

The human licked his lips. "Ward showed up a few hours ago and demanded I get a plane ready."

"Who's Ward?"

"He's some hotshot in Benson Enterprises." The

man confirmed Ice's suspicions that this airfield belonged to their enemies. "I've heard rumors that he's the adopted son of the leader."

"You mean Christopher?"

"Yeah."

Hmm. The Pantera had hoped that when Stanton Locke had been killed by one of his own cohorts, that the betrayal had seriously injured Christopher's organization. Like destroying Robin to hurt Batman.

Now it appeared the bastard had more than one "adopted" son.

"Who was with him?" he demanded.

"Three or four dudes. They stayed outside. I think they were his bodyguards."

"Anyone else?"

The man started to shake his head, only to change his mind when Ice's fingers tightened. "Wait. There was a woman," he confessed. "She was unconscious."

Ice clenched his teeth. It had to be Karen. "Was the woman injured?"

The man hesitated, as if afraid to admit the truth.

"She was bleeding from a cut on her lip," he slowly said.

Ice gave a low growl, his puma restlessly pacing in frustration. His animal wanted blood for blood. His human half, however, understood the need for information. "Where were they going?"

"I don't know." The man screamed as Ice squeezed tight enough to threaten his ability to breathe. "Stop." He coughed as Ice eased his grip. "Their flight plan listed a small airfield south of St. Louis."

St. Louis? Ice scowled in confusion. "Is there a Benson laboratory nearby?"

"I don't know." His expression was pleading. "I swear I don't know. I'm just a grunt. They don't tell me anything."

Ice believed him. This man didn't have the brains to be given sensitive intel. With a flick of his hand, Ice sent the idiot sailing across the room.

"If I were you, I'd look for a new job. Benson Enterprises is about to go out of business," he offered as he turned to leave the hangar.

Cammy was waiting for him beside the Jeep, her stunning eyes shimmering with a violet glow in the sunlight. Ice's cat purred in appreciation, wanting to lick her ivory skin from head to toe.

His musk spiced the air, bringing a blush to her cheeks, but with the rigid composure of a Hunter, she kept her thoughts trained on her duty.

"Tell me what you found out," she commanded.

He halted just inches from her lush form, appreciating her skills as a warrior as much as her intoxicating feminine temptation.

"Nothing more than the fact that they were headed to a small airfield south of St. Louis, and that they had an unconscious woman with them," he said.

She gave a slow nod. "Which means Karen is more than likely a captive and not a mole," she murmured.

He arched a brow. His clever kitty had clearly realized that Karen's disappearance might not have been a simple snatch and grab. If the woman had been spying for Benson Enterprises, her 'kidnapping' might very well have been a ruse used to get her out of the Wildlands without burning her cover.

But it was doubtful they would have gone to the trouble of knocking her unconscious. They couldn't have suspected they'd be followed to the airport.

"Yeah, it appears that way." He shrugged, sharing a glance with Cammy that assured her he intended to stay on guard.

He wasn't taking anyone's innocence for granted.

She nodded in silent agreement, rounded the back of the Jeep and climbed back into the passenger seat.

Ice crawled into his own seat behind the steering wheel, glancing toward the female at his side.

He'd known that he lusted after her lush curves, and that his cat was intrigued with her clever mind and loyalty to her pack. Now he had to add another reason to want to claim Cammy as his own.

They worked as a perfect team.

***

It was one of *those* kinds of dreams.

Cammy released a soft sigh, enjoying the sensual sense of anticipation that shivered through her. She was in a strange room, but she felt perfectly at home as she walked across the soft rug wearing nothing more than a short black robe. It didn't even bother her to know there was a heated gaze watching her from the shadows.

Hell, she preened with the knowledge that she was driving the male crazy with need.

With a sexy twitch of her backside, she moved to crawl onto the chaise longue that was covered in a crimson satin that felt cool against her skin. With a catlike motion she rubbed her cheek against the smooth fabric, the air scented with a familiar male musk.

Raw heat spread through her.

She'd waited for this moment for so long.

Perhaps her entire life. Now she was anxious to lure the predator from the shadows.

"Do you intend to watch, or are you going to join me?" she murmured in a husky voice.

There was a low, male chuckle. Then, with a magic that could only happen in the world of dreams, a hundred candles flickered to life.

Ice prowled into the golden circle of light. "So you want to play, kitty?"

He was wearing nothing more than a loose pair of faded jeans that rode low on his hips. Her mouth went dry as her cat brushed against her inner skin, aching for the touch of his hand.

He was so gorgeous.

Not pretty like Rage. No. He was too raw. Too savagely male.

But he inflamed her senses in a way she'd never dreamed possible.

Which was no doubt the reason she'd tried so hard to keep him at a distance.

Her attraction to Rage had felt safe. Comfortable. Like a well-worn blanket she could wrap around herself.

Certainly it'd never made her heart race or kept her awake at night.

This need for Ice was increasingly wild, threatening to burn out of control.

Thankfully, there was no reason she couldn't indulge her innermost fantasies in her dreams.

Right?

As if she'd abruptly lowered some mental barrier, Ice was moving with fluid speed. She shivered as he perched on the edge of the chaise, his hands braced on each side of her shoulders, trapping her in the corner.

Not that she cared. She wanted to be trapped by this male. Sucking in a deep breath, she savored the exotic spice of his musk.

"Cat got your tongue?" he teased.

Her hand reached up to mold the hard planes of his chest. The heat of his skin seared her palm, making her puma purr in delight. "You were the one to claim that fewer words were better."

A slow, wicked grin curved his lips. "So I did."

Enough.

This was her dream and Cammy was done waiting for what she wanted.

Jerking his head down, she sighed in relief as he claimed her mouth in a fierce kiss. Heat sizzled through her, making her toes curl. Her cat hissed, pressing beneath her skin in wicked pleasure.

She heard him release a low growl as his tongue swept between her lips, thrusting in a slow rhythm that clenched her stomach with an aching need.

Instinctively she arched closer to the hardness of his body. She needed more.

She needed his hard length deep inside her.

"Ice," she breathed as his lips burned a trail of kisses down the curve of her neck.

"Is this what you want?" he murmured, his

fingers skimming down her body to grasp the belt of her robe. With one tug he had it undone and was pulling aside the silky material, and with a blatant possession he was cupping her breasts.

"Yes," she encouraged, her heart pounding as his thumbs teased her nipples to tight buds.

"How about this?" His lips traced the line of her collarbone, moving down to nuzzle the curve of her breasts.

With a muttered sound of pleasure he lapped at the tip of her nipple. Cammy's pussy clenched at the rough rasp of his tongue over her sensitive flesh.

Dear Goddess. She was ready to orgasm.

"Please." Her nails dug into his chest. "I want you."

"I know, Cammy," he muttered, abruptly moving until he was off the chaise and kneeling between her legs.

Cammy tried to pull him back, but evading her hands, he was quickly stripping her out of her robe. Okay. She liked where he was going with this.

Shrugging out of the sleeves, she allowed him to tug aside the flimsy material. Then, studying him with half-closed eyes, she groaned in encouragement when his clever fingers traced her naked body with gentle care.

Oh yeah. He obviously knew precisely what he was doing.

Was he this skilled in reality?

She was betting he was. Ice was a male who appreciated being the best.

At *all* things.

"Christ, you're beautiful," he breathed before he

was leaning forward to tug one hardened nipple into his mouth.

Cammy's breath hissed between her clenched teeth. She'd had a variety of sexual fantasies. She might have thought she was destined for Rage, but she liked to imagine a variety of males in her dreams.

But not one of them had ever aroused the savage hunger that was making her squirm beneath his touch.

Who could ever have suspected the badass Ice could be the one to set her on fire?

Her fingers clutched at his hair as she felt the rasp of his whispers against her sensitive flesh.

"I'm glad this is a dream," she whispered.

"Why?" He moved his lips to her other breast, teasing the hard bud with his teeth before closing his lips over it.

Cammy moaned as he leaned heavily against her, his body pressed to the juncture of her legs. With every movement he brushed against her tender clit, sending jolts of electric excitement through her.

Her hands restlessly moved to stroke over his shoulders, delighting in the feel of his hard, rippling muscles beneath her fingers. He was so solid, so strong.

So real.

"You terrify me."

"Cammy," he moaned, lifting his head to bury his lips in the curve of her neck. "I would never hurt you."

His breath whispered against her skin even as she felt his fingers stroke down the tense plane of her stomach and over the curve of her hip. Cammy shivered, a shocking heat streaking through her.

"No, but you would consume me."

He chuckled. "Oh yeah, kitty. Awake or asleep, I'm going to consume you."

She nearly jumped off the sofa as his searching hand at last reached the bare skin of her thighs. *Yes, yes, yes.* She was on fire. As if her blood had turned to molten lava.

Claiming her lips in a devouring kiss, Ice continued his soft caresses. His fingers stroking higher and higher. And abruptly he found the moist heat of her pussy.

Cammy cried out in delight a second before he was covering her mouth with a deep, possessive kiss. Her cat roared with furious pleasure, the dark hunger threatening to overwhelm her.

She grasped at his arms, her fingers digging into his flesh as she instinctively arched against his invading touch.

With a slow thrust he pressed his finger deeper, using his thumb to rub against her sensitive clit. Pressure was building deep inside her as his finger slid in and out of her. A delicious, aching pressure that was threatening to shatter at any second.

"Ice...please," she husked. She desperately wanted to feel his hard body covering her as he thrust deep inside.

With a wicked expertise, Ice trailed a path of searing kisses down her neck. He used the tip of his tongue to trace the line of her collarbone. The rhythm of his finger quickened as she moaned. And dipping his head downward, he latched his mouth onto the tip of her breast and sucked with sweet insistence.

Oblivious to everything but the sensations that seared through her, Cammy wrapped her legs about Ice's waist, her entire body arching. She was hovering on the crest of paradise.

His thumb pressed just right on her clit, and for a heart-stopping minute the world came to a halt. A perfect moment out of time. Then with a magical stroke of his fingers she was hurtled over the edge and a cry of startled bliss was wrenched from her throat.

Oh hell.

That had been glorious.

Still shaking from the force of her climax, Cammy did her best to ignore the persistent sound of her name being whispered in her ear.

Dammit, she was enjoying the moment. Why wouldn't Ice leave her in peace?

Slowly the fog of pleasure began to fade and Cammy realized it wasn't her dream Ice whispering in her ear, but a very real Ice.

Wrenching herself awake, she opened her eyes to find that she was snuggled into the passenger seat of the Jeep, with Ice leaning close enough she could feel the brush of his warm breath over her cheeks.

Her face flushed with a sudden heat.

Not embarrassment at being wakened from a sex dream, but by a flare of primal desire. It was as if her erotic fantasies had only intensified her need for a male.

No. Not a male.

For Ice.

Unnerved by the realization, Cammy abruptly straightened in her seat, desperately trying to put space between them.

"Sorry, I didn't mean to fall asleep," she muttered, turning her attention to their surroundings. Anything to avoid his piercing blue gaze.

"You didn't miss anything," he murmured, his voice oddly husky as he reached to tuck a loose curl behind her ear.

She refused to glance in his direction. There was already the risk he could catch the scent of her arousal. She didn't want him to see the heat of her cat in her eyes. "I could have helped to drive."

Turning off the engine, he shoved open his door. "Do you think I'm a male who ever rides in the passenger seat?"

Her tension dissipated as he deliberately lightened the mood, clearly aware of her unease and hoping to make her comfortable. The knowledge allowed her to turn and send him a teasing smirk.

"See, I told you...an arrogant ass."

He laughed, climbing out of the Jeep and waiting for her to grab her backpack and join him at the front of the vehicle.

"I need to stretch my legs," he said. "And if I don't get something hot in my stomach I'm going to pass out."

On cue, Cammy's stomach rumbled with hunger. While she'd been sleeping, the entire day had passed. Now she realized she was starving.

"Where are we?" she demanded, glancing around the dense woodlands that surrounded a large, rustic cabin with a sloped roof and wraparound porch.

He waved a hand toward the trees. "We're in the middle of a wildlife refuge in southern Missouri."

Placing a hand on her lower back, he urged her up the narrow pathway. "The cabin belongs to Belise. I called her to see if we could use it to rest for an hour or two."

The name sent an odd stab of annoyance through Cammy. Which was ridiculous. She barely knew the female Diplomat. Well, she knew that she was beautiful. And sophisticated. And that most of the males were making idiots of themselves to attract her attention whenever she spent time in the Wildlands.

Did that include Ice?

Climbing onto the porch, she stepped to the side, dislodging his lingering hand. Ice sent her a puzzled glance, then turned his attention to the electronic pad where he punched in the private code.

The door swung open and Cammy stepped inside, her eyes widening at the sight of the elegant furnishings and the priceless antique ornaments displayed in glass cases.

"Wow," she breathed.

"Yeah," Ice agreed, stepping in behind her. "My cousin enjoys the finer things in life. She was based in Paris before returning stateside."

Cammy blinked in surprise. "Cousin?"

He brushed a hand down her back. "You didn't know?"

She shook her head, and with a smug chuckle that should've pissed her off, he moved toward the door leading into the kitchen.

"I'm not sure I know anything about you beyond the fact you traveled with your parents, and that Parish considers you to be one of his most trusted Hunters."

His fingers cupped her hip, subtly drawing her

closer to his hard body as they came to a halt in the center of the tiled floor.

"I assumed you weren't interested," he murmured, his brooding gaze sweeping over her face. "Has that changed?"

Cammy shivered, sensing that something *had* changed.

She just didn't know what the hell it was.

"I…" Her words trailed away as she bit her lip.

Thankfully he sensed her distress, and with a wry smile he urged her toward the nearby breakfast bar.

"Belise promised the freezer was fully stocked," he said. "Have a seat at the table and I'll cook us a couple of steaks."

He cooked?

With a sigh, Cammy took her seat and watched as the luscious male moved around the kitchen with a competent ease. She was in trouble.

Big, big trouble.

CHAPTER 4

Karen was prepared when the male voice spoke to her from the shadows.

"Did you enjoy your dinner?" the mystery man asked.

Karen pasted a smile onto her lips. During the endless hours waiting for the return of her captor she'd come to the decision that her only hope was trying to forge a personal connection. Unlike the last time she'd been kidnapped, this male wasn't treating her as if she was a lump of flesh they needed for their sick experiments. He talked to her as if she was a real woman.

I was a long shot, but she might actually be able to convince him to let her out of the cage.

From there...well, one step at a time.

"It was delicious. Thank you," she murmured, rising from the cot to stand at the door of the cage. She was still weak, and her head still throbbed, but she was capable of standing thanks to the truly delicious food that had been delivered during the day. "I still don't know your name."

There was a long silence before he at last answered. "Ward."

"Ward," she slowly repeated the name. It wasn't familiar, but that wasn't surprising. Few of her captors had ever bothered to introduce themselves. "Do I know you? From before?"

His weird laugh echoed through the empty space. "You could say that."

Karen frowned. She sensed a double meaning in his words, but she didn't get it.

"Why won't you show me your face?" she asked.

"Because I want us to become better acquainted first," he abruptly snapped.

Karen grabbed the bars, hiding her flare of impatience behind a tight smile. The man seemed twitchy. As if he might shut down the conversation at any moment. It was up to her to keep him there and talking.

"Okay," she soothed in gentle tones. "What do you want to know?"

There was a shuffle of feet as if he'd stepped closer to the door. "Why did you run away?"

"Run away?" She blinked in confusion.

"When you were working for Benson laboratories," he muttered. "You simply disappeared."

Was he kidding?

She gave a slow shake of her head. "I didn't run away. Indy came and helped me escape. I was being held as a prisoner."

She heard his sharply indrawn breath. "Don't say that."

Karen's confusion deepened. "Say what?"

"That you were a prisoner."

"Why shouldn't I?" she asked. "It's the truth."

"No. You were a volunteer, not a prisoner."

Karen flinched as if she'd been slapped. Just for a moment she suspected he was cruelly taunting her. Did he take pleasure in pretending she hadn't been kidnapped, abused, and tortured for over ten years?

"I'm not sure who told you that, but I was kidnapped at the age of seventeen when I was walking home from school," she said, forcing her voice to remain calm despite the ugly emotions twisting her gut into a knot. "They snatched me off the streets and threw me in a cage."

There was more shuffling, almost as if the man was battling against his urge to storm into the lab.

"I've read your file," he said, his voice vibrating with a hint of a growl. Was he Pantera? Or maybe a hybrid? "It says that you arrived at Benson Enterprises and pleaded to be taken in as a volunteer. It said your mother was abusive—"

"My mother would never have hurt me," she angrily interrupted. She wouldn't allow anyone to spread nasty stories about her beloved mother.

Even if it meant putting herself in danger.

Clearly frustrated by her refusal to play his game, the man slammed his fist loudly against the open door. "Stop it," he snarled. "Why do you lie?"

Karen frowned. He truly believed what he was saying. The mystery man thought she'd happily agreed to become a brood mare and could have waltzed away whenever she wanted.

Sucking in a deep breath, she shoved her arm through the steel bars, stretching her hand out in a pleading motion.

"I'm telling the truth, Ward," she swore. "Whoever wrote the file you were reading was spreading lies."

"I don't believe you," he hissed between clenched teeth. "You volunteered, but after you had children you grew tired of being in the lab. You took your favorite child and walked away."

"Never," she rasped. "Never, never, never."

"You did," he insisted, sounding like a petulant kid.

Karen swayed, her eyes squeezing shut.

"Listen to me. I would never leave my children," she insisted, her voice thick with pain. How dare he imply that she'd ever abandon her babies? There wasn't a night that passed that she didn't cry out in agony, the hole in the center of her heart never healing. "After I gave birth, my sons were taken from me. I wasn't even allowed to hold them. It broke my heart, but thankfully Indy arrived to release me from my cage," she said. She'd been so close to giving up on all hope when young Indy had boldly crept into the lab and released her. "I found Caleb strapped to a gurney, being treated like a…" Her voice broke at the heart-wrenching memory of Caleb bound by leather bands, his scrawny body barely more than skin and bones and his hair matted with filth. Even more astonishing had been the rapid rate of his growth. Until she'd finally gotten him to the Wildlands he'd been maturing almost twice as fast as a normal human. No doubt a reaction to his Pantera DNA. "I searched for my other sons, but I couldn't find them. So we released all the prisoners we could find and torched the lab."

"And now you've started a new life," he drawled, obviously not impressed with her story.

"I've done my best to start over," she hesitantly agreed. What did he want from her?

Again he slammed his fist into the door. "Forgetting those you left behind."

She shook her head. "I would never forget my sons. They're my heart."

"Easy to say," he rasped.

Karen abruptly stiffened. Dear god. Was it possible…?

Grabbing the bars of the cage, she gave the door a frustrated shake. "Do you know where I can find them?" she demanded. "Do you know my sons?"

There was a long, excruciating silence before he at last answered. "Yes."

"Oh, dear god." Her knees threatened to buckle at the intense relief that seared through her. "Tell me what you know. Please. I'll do anything you ask. Anything."

As if her desperate pleas had at last stirred the mystery man into action, there was a ripple of movement and he stepped into the lab.

Karen had a confused second when she accepted the male was a stranger.

He looked to be in his early twenties, with the lean, muscular body of many Pantera, covered by an expensive gray suit. Then the fluorescent lights caught the red highlights in his closely trimmed hair and shimmered in the green eyes.

Her heart refused to beat as she took in the pale, elegant features that were almost an exact match to Caleb's.

Oh dear lord…

Her knees collapsed as the world went black. With a soft groan, Karen tumbled onto the hard floor.

***

Ice tried to concentrate on keeping the Jeep on increasingly narrow roads as Cammy directed him through the darkness.

A task that was much more difficult than it should have been.

Dammit. He should have used their rest stop at the cabin to talk to her. It's what he'd intended to do. After all, he was well aware that she'd spent the afternoon dreaming of him.

He'd caught the unmistakable scent of her arousal even as she'd softly whispered his name.

But he hadn't missed her wary glances, or the way she'd kept a physical distance between them. She might be slowly accepting that she was sexually attracted to him, but she still battled against the deeper awareness that was forming.

His cat urged him to pounce, but his human heart warned that pressing her too far, too fast might ruin any hope of earning her as his mate.

Besides, they were on a mission to track down their enemies and retrieve one of their kidnapped packmates.

Not precisely the time or place to reveal his innermost feelings.

But as they neared their destination, Ice felt a knot of regret in the pit of his stomach.

He'd wasted years. First, by trying ignore his feelings for her. And then by being too cowardly to make his claim.

Was he really willing to walk into danger without telling Cammy how he felt, and what he wanted from her?

"Turn left on the next road," Cammy said, interrupting his inner thoughts. "She should be just ahead."

His decision made, Ice forced himself to concentrate on their surroundings.

For the past hour they'd been driving through empty farmland, but as Ice turned the Jeep down the road that had been recently graveled, his night-gaze caught sight of the outline of distant buildings.

Pulling to a halt, he leaned forward, studying the high chain-link fence that framed the industrial compound. He could make out a three-storied central building made of concrete blocks, with several smaller structures that looked like barracks. At the far end there was a runway with a metal hangar.

"It looks like an abandoned military facility," he murmured.

"Not entirely abandoned," Cammy said, nodding toward the prop plane sitting near the hangar. "Someone's here."

Ice glanced toward the fence. Even at a distance he could make out the cameras tucked into the barbed wire at the top. He could also see tiny sensors that he assumed were motion detectors. It wouldn't be easy to approach without being noticed.

"We need to do a sweep to check the security before we try to enter," he warned.

Cammy leaned down, pulling her handgun from the backpack at her feet.

"I'll head to the south and meet you on the other side," she said, instantly in warrior mode.

His body tingled with male appreciation. Was there anything sexier than a strong, beautiful female?

He reached out as she shoved open her door, grasping her upper arm. "Wait."

She glanced back in confusion. "What's wrong?"

He allowed his fingers to stroke upward, tracing the line of her shoulder. "I want to say something before we do this."

Her eyes dilated with arousal at his light caress, but her expression was wary. "Ice—"

He interrupted her protest. "Please." He wasn't going to be stopped. Not this time.

She licked her lips, making him instantly hard. He'd spent more than a few hours fantasizing about having that lush mouth wrapped around his cock.

"What?"

His fingers traced the vulnerable curve of her throat, resting over the rapid beat of her pulse.

"When Parish requested that I return to the Wildlands, I resisted," he admitted, the musk of his puma scenting the air. The animal inside him didn't understand why he wasn't pouncing on this female to physically prove he was stronger and more cunning than any other potential mate. It didn't want to talk. It wanted to lick and bite and taste every luscious inch of Cammy before pinning her beneath him so he could take her with a wild hunger. "My parents often traveled to dangerous locations around the world and I felt it was my duty to protect them."

She stilled, as if captivated by his soft words. "What made you change your mind?"

"You."

Her eyes widened. "Me?"

His lips twitched at her blatant disbelief. He'd clearly done a better job than he thought at hiding his obsession with her.

"Trust me, I tried to fight it," he said in wry tones. "But from the first time I caught sight of you I was fascinated."

She shook her head, her pulse leaping beneath his fingertips. "You glared at me all the time."

He grimaced, recalling the petty jealousy that'd plagued him for so long.

"Because you were panting over Rage," he muttered.

A flush stained her cheeks. "I never panted."

"You did," Ice insisted, his voice a growl. The mere thought of Cammy being with another male was enough to make him conjure homicidal thoughts. "You wanted to be with him."

She paused, visibly considering whether or not to tell him the truth.

"I don't know if it's what I wanted, or what I thought I should want," she at last confessed in tones so low he barely caught the words.

He arched his brows. "What you thought you should want?"

"Rage has been my best friend since we were cubs. He always felt comfortable."

"And you don't feel comfortable with me?"

Her answer came without hesitation. "No."

"Good." He lowered his head, kissing her with a fierce surge of joy. He didn't want her comfortable with him. He wanted her excited and aroused and breathless when he walked into a room. That's how he felt every time she was near. "I'm not sure how many times I was forced to leash my desire to punch Rage in his handsome face."

She bit her bottom lip, her eyes glowing as her cat responded to his kiss. Her puma wasn't conflicted. It wanted him.

Now.

"He's really a very good guy and a dedicated Hunter," she said, a shiver racing through her body.

"Maybe." He shrugged. "But he was a competitor for your attention. Which meant my primitive side could only see him as the enemy," he admitted with brutal honesty.

"And now?"

His gaze locked on her lips. "Now I don't intend to punch him."

"I'm sure he'll be pleased."

His hands cupped her face, his gaze holding hers as the air heated with his searing hunger. "And I don't intend to waste any more time waiting for you to notice me," he growled with unmistakable determination.

She gave a breathless laugh. "Trust me, I've noticed."

He stole another kiss, savoring the lush satin of her. His thumbs traced the line of her jaw, tilting back her head as he dipped his tongue between her lips. He groaned at the sweet taste of her feminine desire.

"Keep noticing," he murmured, brushing his mouth over the silken heat of her cheek.

She trembled, her hands lifting to clutch at his shoulders. "Ice."

"No." He nipped her lower lip. "I don't need you to say anything. I just wanted you to know that my cat is done waiting. He wants to be on the hunt."

She pulled back, her expression impossible to read. "What if I'm not ready?"

"Then I get to enjoy stalking you," he said, his cat not at all opposed to spending time playing with his prey. There were few things he liked better than a challenge. He studied her pale face. "Just tell me one thing."

"What?"

"Are you scared of me?"

She blinked, seemingly caught off guard by his question.

"You can be intimidating," she slowly said. "And arrogant. And mysterious. But no." She gave a decisive shake of her head. "You don't scare me."

His cat roared with satisfaction.

The chase was on.

"That's all I need to know." With a last, lingering kiss he released his hold on her. "Are you ready?"

Her lips parted, then, clearly deciding now wasn't the time to finish their conversation, she slid out of the Jeep. "Let's go."

***

Karen came back to consciousness with a sudden jolt.

Snapping open her eyes, she realized she was lying on the hard floor in her cage. But she wasn't alone.

Trying to think through the fog in her brain, she cleared her throat. "What happened?"

"You passed out." The man suddenly crouched beside her, his hair tousled as if he'd been running his fingers through the short strands.

Suddenly Karen remembered exactly what had sent her tumbling into darkness.

"Oh," she breathed, her hand trembling as she lifted it to press against his lean face. "Ward." She tested his name on her tongue. "You're my son."

He gave a slow nod, his tension a tangible force in the air. "Yes."

"You're as handsome as I dreamed." She released a pained laugh, trying to absorb the realization that this was truly her son. She'd tried to imagine what he would look like a thousand times, but she'd always thought of him as a nine-year-old boy with skinned knees and a goofy grin. Not a grown man. "Although considerably older," she wryly admitted.

"My Pantera blood makes me age at an accelerated rate," he said, his tone absent and his brow furrowed. Clearly his inner thoughts were troubling him. "My master has assured me my lifespan will still be much longer than a mere human."

She nodded. It was the same way with Caleb, although his aging had slowed since they'd moved to the Wildlands. She assumed it had something to do with the magic of the bayous.

"Master?" She grimaced. "You mean Christopher?"

"Yes. He became my adoptive father after you abandoned me," he said.

With a flurry of movement, Karen was pushing herself to her feet, fury pulsing through her. It wasn't enough that the head of Benson Enterprises had kidnapped her and used her as a brood mare before snatching away her babies? Now she discovered that he'd brainwashed her own son into believing he was some sort of hero instead of the villain.

"That bastard," she hissed through clenched teeth. Then, with an effort, she regained command of her composure. "What about your brother?" she demanded. "Was he adopted by Christopher?"

Ward gave a shake of his head. "No. I've searched the records, but I couldn't find more than the proof that he was born in New York."

Karen grimaced, squashing her sharp disappointment. "Why would they separate you?"

"I don't know." He shrugged. "I can't be sure he's still alive."

"He's alive. I can feel him." Karen pressed a hand to her heart, her expression fierce. "Here."

"I hope you're right, but I have no way of finding him." Straightening, Ward smoothed his hands down the expensive fabric of his jacket.

Karen tried to tell herself she should be pleased that her son had clearly not been mistreated. In fact, it appeared he'd been given a position of authority in the corporation. Unfortunately, that didn't stop her from wanting to put a bullet through Christopher's black heart.

"Is it true?" he abruptly demanded.

She frowned. "That you're my son?"

He gave an impatient shake of his head. "That you were held against your will."

Karen held his accusing gaze, sensing that deep down he'd always suspected he wasn't being told the entire truth.

"I have proof," she assured him, slowly pulling up the sleeves of her sweater to reveal the thick scars that marred her wrists. "These are from the handcuffs they kept on me even after the skin was rubbed so raw my wounds became infected." She pushed aside her hair to point toward the raised flesh on the side of her neck. "This is the brand they put on me so the doctors would know I was a breeder." She shivered, still able to remember the searing pain. Then, she tugged at her neckline to reveal the ugly round spot in the center of her chest. "This is the mark from the cigarette the guard seared into my flesh because he didn't like how I was looking at him."

Ward's face drained to a shade of ash as he lifted his hand. "Enough," he croaked.

Karen caught a brief glimpse of pain in his eyes and had to blink back a fresh batch of tears. The thought that she'd been hurt bothered him. Which meant he had to care. Right? Even if he'd been told lie after lie, he still thought of her as his mother.

"I would never have left you." Her hand again lifted, compulsively touching his face. She had to reassure herself that he was real. "You were snatched from my arms and I've spent years trying to find you."

Confusion darkened his eyes. "Why would he lie to me?"

She cupped his cheek, joy racing through her. After all the years of longing, she was at last touching her son. It was…glorious.

"We can find the answer together, Ward," she assured him, glancing toward the door of the cell that he'd left open. Obviously he'd been worried when she'd fainted and hadn't bothered to lock it. "But first we need to get out of here."

He took a sharp step backward, his brows snapping together. "And go where? Back to the animals?"

She swallowed the urge to point out that the 'animals' had acted far more humanely than the humans. Right now all that mattered was getting him away from the lab so they could talk without fear of interruption.

"We can go anywhere you want. We can get Caleb from my cabin and we'll—"

"Someone's coming." Ward interrupted her fierce words, his nose flaring as he sniffed the air. Proof his senses were far more acute than hers. "Pantera."

Relief flared through her. They'd come for her. She hadn't dared to hope that they would consider her important enough to risk a rescue mission.

Then her relief was replaced by a jolt of fear as her son reached beneath his jacket to pull out a handgun.

"No." She grabbed his arms, her expression desperate. "They're not your enemy, Ward. I swear."

***

Ice led Cammy down the narrow flight of stairs into the hidden labyrinth of rooms that were connected by long hallways lined with stainless steel. She was convinced that Karen was near. Unfortunately, there was no way to get to her without taking the main corridor.

Moving in silence, they were both on full alert. Slowing as they reached a branch in the corridor, Ice waited for Cammy to point toward the right.

"That way," she whispered.

About to head down the hallway, Ice reached around to lightly touch his companion's arm. "Wait here," he murmured. "I'll be right back."

She frowned in confusion. "Where are you going?"

"To have some fun."

Without giving her time to protest, he spun on his heel and retraced his steps to the staircase. He could smell the two humans approaching.

Pressing his large body against the wall, he stood predator-still in the shadows of the steps. He didn't bother to draw his gun. At close range, he could kill easier with his hands. And it was considerably quieter.

After spending nearly a half hour bypassing the Pentagon-grade security surrounding the compound, the last thing he wanted was to alert anyone to their presence.

Unaware of the danger, the two men entered the hallway. Ice allowed them to walk past him before he stepped from the shadows and grabbed them by the back of their necks. With a low grunt, he lifted them off the floor, ignoring the startled curses. Both men struggled to escape the punishing grip of his fingers, but using the narrow hallway to his advantage, Ice shoved out his arms and smashed their faces into the walls. Grunts of pain replaced their cursing, the dull thud of their skulls connecting with the stainless steel echoing through the hallway. Ice felt them go limp, but he continued to smack them against the wall until the pungent scent of blood filled the air.

Only then did he drag their unconscious bodies into a janitorial closet and shut the door. Assuming the guards did a consistent route, they wouldn't be missed for at least ten or fifteen minutes.

In that time he and Cammy should be able to grab Karen and get the hell out of there.

With a last glance to make sure he hadn't missed any security cameras, Ice hurried back to Cammy who, with an arch of her brow, studied the blood that had dripped onto his boots.

"Happy?"

He allowed a smug smile to curve his lips. It hadn't been entirely satisfying. After the bastards had directly attacked the Wildlands he was eager to punish their enemies. But at least he'd had the chance to bust a few heads.

"It will have to do for now," he murmured.

She rolled her eyes, heading down the hallway. "Karen's in the last room at the end." She paused as they reached the door, sucking in a deep breath of air. "There's one guard inside."

Anticipation raced through his body. "I'll take care of him."

She grabbed his arm. "Hey, I should have some fun too."

He flashed a wicked grin. "I promise that when we have some time alone I'll give you all the fun you can handle."

"Yeesh." She glared at him, even as her lips twitched at his teasing. "We go in together," she asserted.

"Fine." Ice's amusement faded as he slid the gun from his holster. There would be no way to sneak up on this guard. "Cover me."

Cammy positioned herself at his side, pointing her weapon as he pushed open the door.

Ice had a split second to study the tall, lean man with short reddish hair and eyes that glowed with power before Karen was abruptly darting in front of him.

He scowled, unable to get a clear shot.

"Karen, move," he snapped, wondering if the woman had been drugged.

"No, don't shoot," she pleaded.

Ice felt Cammy lay a restraining hand on his arm. "What's going on, Karen?" she demanded.

"This is Ward," she said in soft tones. "My son."

Ice studied the man's lean face and green eyes. It was easy to see the family resemblance now that he was looking for it. "The one you've been searching for?" he demanded.

"Yes."

Ward grasped his mother by her shoulders, tugging her to the side. His gaze flickered between Cammy and Ice. "Who are you?"

It was Cammy who answered. "Friends of your mother."

The male snorted. "Pantera have never been friends to humans."

Ice tilted back his head, sniffing the air. He'd caught

the hint of musk the moment he'd stepped into the room. "You're as much an animal as I am," he taunted.

The younger male stiffened. "I might have Pantera blood, but I'm not a savage. We all know you're determined to kill the hybrids."

Ice's brows snapped together at the accusation. "Don't be stupid. Why would we destroy our own people?"

Karen turned toward her son, her hand settling lightly on his shoulder. "He's telling you the truth, Ward. The Pantera have welcomed all people into their pack. Including humans."

He stepped away from her touch, his expression wary as he focused on Ice. Like most humans—or Pantera raised in the human world—he no doubt assumed Ice was the more lethal. The idiot clearly didn't realize that Cammy could rip him apart with her bare hands.

"How can I believe you?" Ward demanded.

Ice ignored the question. He wasn't without sympathy for Karen, but his duty was to rescue her and return home. It wasn't to convince her son that they weren't evil savages. Still, he hesitated.

The male might have information. Beginning with whether or not Benson Enterprises was declaring open war on the Pantera, or if it'd been a mere ploy so Ward could get his hands on his mother.

"Why did you come to the Wildlands?" he abruptly demanded.

The male hesitated before giving a tilt of his chin. "I discovered my mother was there, along with my half-brother. I wanted to know why she'd left me."

"So you sent in a suicide bomber to destroy us?" he snapped.

Karen made a sound of distress, her eyes darkening with genuine concern. "Oh my god. I thought I heard an explosion. Was anyone hurt?"

Ice's jaw tightened at the memory of the chaotic fear that'd been spread through his homeland. The Wildlands had always offered a sense of peace to his people, even when it was being destroyed by Shakpi. It was the one place they would always be safe.

That'd been stolen from them by their enemies.

"There were injuries, but no fatalities, thank the Goddess," he said, his gaze locked on the young male. "Not that they didn't intend to kill as many of us as possible."

Ward lifted a slender hand. "That wasn't me."

Ice narrowed his gaze. "You had nothing to do with it?"

The male hesitated, no doubt trying to decide if he wanted to tell the truth or not. At last he gave a lift of one shoulder.

"I knew it was planned, so I took the opportunity to slip in and bring my mother here," he admitted.

Ice's lips parted to demand why they'd been attacked, only to be interrupted by the sharp sound of an alarm ripping through the air.

Shit. The guards had been missed.

Karen paled. "What's that?"

"Trouble," Ward muttered, holstering the gun he probably thought Ice hadn't noticed before he was turning to head toward the back of the room. "Follow me. I can get you to the escape tunnels."

"Wait," Ice commanded as Karen moved to join her son. "This could be a trap."

Ward sent him an impatient glare. "The alarm has sounded which means they know you're here. The facility is on full lockdown," he warned. "You'll never get out unless you come with me."

Ice scowled. His acute hearing had picked up the sound of locks clicking in place. That didn't make him any more trusting of Ward and his sudden eagerness to help them escape.

"Fine." He pointed his gun directly at the male's head. "But remember this. I'm not your mother. I won't hesitate to shoot you in the head if I sense you're leading us into danger."

"Savage," the male muttered, laying his palm on a small scanner set on the back wall. Silently a panel slid to the side, revealing a narrow corridor. "This way."

Allowing Ward to take the lead, Ice indicated for Karen to go next, and then Cammy, while he brought up the rear.

***

Cammy didn't miss Ice's piercing gaze as she passed by him to enter the corridor. He intended to remain on alert for any danger. It was now her duty to take the lead on discovering what Ward knew about Benson Enterprises' plans for the Pantera.

Ice slid the panel shut behind them, wrapping them in darkness. Cammy instinctively stepped beside Karen to wrap an arm around her waist. The human woman didn't possess the same night vision as a Pantera. Ward, however, moved with an ease that proved he was as much cat as he was human.

"You said that you weren't involved with the suicide bomber," she said, her voice pitched low to keep from echoing through the long, empty space.

"I wasn't," Ward muttered, his attention locked on the darkness in front of them as he moved forward at a swift pace. "I only used the distraction to enter the Wildlands."

Easy enough to claim. "Then what was the purpose of the bomber?"

Ward paused, his body tensed as he abruptly turned to lead them into a side corridor. "He was trying to destroy the computers you stole."

Cammy frowned. Over the past few months they'd managed to track down a handful of Benson Enterprise labs. Xavier always insisted the Hunters bring back any intel that might help to discover more about the enemy before the Pantera torched the buildings. But none of the computers they'd confiscated had seemed worth such an extreme response.

"Why?" she demanded.

The male said nothing as they hurried down the hallway. At last Karen reached out blindly, brushing her hand over her son's back.

"Ward, we need to know," she murmured in a soft voice.

"There's private research that they didn't want falling into your hands," he at last muttered, the words sounding as if they were being forced past his stiff lips.

Clearly his loyalty was being divided between his employers and the woman who'd given him life.

"What sort of research?" Cammy pressed.

He shook his head, his shoulders hunched. "I can't."

Again Karen reached out to touch Ward's back. "Please. It's important that the Pantera know how to protect themselves."

There was a long silence before Ward at last heaved a loud sigh. "Dammit." His steps slowed as he glanced over his shoulder. "Christopher is creating a virus."

Cammy blinked in confusion. "A computer virus?"

"No. A biological virus."

Stunned, Cammy struggled not to trip over her feet. She was a Hunter, not a Healer, but she knew enough to feel a tight knot of dread settle in the pit of her stomach.

Obviously sharing her concern, Ice moved until he was at her side, filling the narrow hallway with the prickling heat of his power.

"Why?" Ice growled.

Ward was forced to halt as he reached a steel door that blocked the hallway. Reaching out, he pressed his hand against a glass panel set in the wall. "Christian realized after the Pantera discovered his connection to Benson Enterprises that he's been put in a vulnerable position," he said, his voice stripped of emotion. "He demanded that his scientists come up with a fail-safe in case things go south."

Cammy could feel the tension that clenched Ice's body.

"What's the fail-safe?" she demanded.

"A lethal disease that's mutated to kill the Pantera," Ward muttered.

Dear Goddess. He was talking about a custom-designed pandemic meant to wipe out her entire species.

What sort of monster would even contemplate such a horrendous crime?

Sickness rolled through her, and Cammy instinctively reached to touch Ice's arm. The last thing she wanted was to interfere in his ability to fight, but she desperately needed the comfort of his warm, strong presence.

"Has he already created the virus?" Ice rasped.

"I don't know for sure, but the files were on the computer that was stolen from the lab in Bossier City," Ward explained. "Christopher is desperate to make sure the Pantera don't have access to the research."

The door slid open and Ward led them into what looked like a small storage room. The male stepped into the cramped space, waiting for the rest of them to squeeze inside before he turned to close the door. At the same time the deafening sound of gunshots splintered the air.

Hissing in pain, Ward dropped to his knees, his hand pressed to his chest. Karen cried out, rushing forward before Cammy could stop her.

Crouching down, she wrapped an arm around Ward's shoulders as she tried to see through the darkness. "Have you been hit?"

"I'm fine," Ward hissed through gritted teeth. "Get back."

Cammy leaped forward at the same time as Ice, but before they could reach Karen there was another barrage of gunfire that sent them diving for the floor. Cammy crawled forward, her heart missing a beat as Karen fell to the side, a bloody gouge marring her right temple.

Shit.

With the last of his strength, Ward reached out to slam shut the door, bringing a temporary end to the flying bullets. Then, with a groan, he leaned against the wall, his shirt covered with blood.

"There's a tunnel behind the shelves. It leads beneath the fence," he said, his voice husky with pain. "I'll keep them from following as long as I can."

Ice rose to his feet. "The virus—"

"I truly don't know any more than I've told you," Ward interrupted, his face bathed in sweat as he continued to bleed out at an alarming rate. He glanced toward the woman who was lying unconscious next to him. "Take my mother and keep her safe." He pulled his gun from beneath his jacket, his face grim. None of them needed to be Healers to know that he wasn't going to survive long enough for them to get him to a doctor. "Go."

Moving forward, Cammy grabbed Karen around the waist and tossed her over her shoulder before she was straightening. Ice hesitated, no doubt consumed with the need to discover more about the virus that had the potential to destroy them. But the sound of footsteps outside the door had him spinning around with a curse.

With blinding speed he had the shelves shoved

aside, revealing the tunnel. Cammy didn't hesitate as she darted forward, entering the dark, moldy passageway with Karen still slung across her shoulder. They could only hope that Ward would be helped by his guards.

Right now nothing mattered beyond getting out of the compound so they could warn Raphael of the newest danger to their people.

CHAPTER 5

It felt like an eternity had passed before Ice could at last give in to the fierce instincts of his puma.

First, it'd been the silent drive back to the Wildlands. Then, leaving Karen in the capable hands of the Healers, they'd sought out Raphael and Parish to reveal what Ward had told them. Next, Xavier, the head of the Geeks, had demanded an opportunity to grill them for information.

They were all on edge with this latest threat, and it'd been difficult to find an opportunity to spend time alone with Cammy. Now, however, he refused to be put off any longer.

Shifting into his cat form, Ice ran through the Wildlands, his animal roaring with pleasure as he worked off the edge of his frustration before he was heading to the small cabin near the edge of the communal center. His lips twitched as he shifted back to human. Trust Cammy to be in the middle of the action.

His own cabin was built in the middle of a distant bog, far from his nearest neighbor.

They would have to find some way to compromise.

Giving a sharp knock on the door, he released a

soft purr as Cammy pulled open the door. It was past midnight, allowing him to appreciate her lush beauty brushed with silver in the moonlight.

Her thick hair was tumbled around her shoulders, her amazing violet eyes glowing with the awareness of her cat. Her feminine curves were outlined by the satin robe that was belted around her slender waist.

Glorious.

"Hello, Cammy," he murmured, leaning against the doorjamb.

She arched her brow, her gaze taking a slow survey of his casual jeans and sweatshirt.

"It's late," she murmured.

"Not that late." He reached out to lightly touch her cheek. "How's Karen?"

Cammy grimaced. She'd left the meeting with Raphael saying that she wanted to visit the clinic before she went home.

"Physically she'll heal in a few days. The bullet only grazed her temple," she said. "Emotionally, she's a wreck."

Ice gave a slow nod. They had no way of knowing if Ward had survived. He had Pantera blood, but all hybrids were different. And they had no way of knowing if the guards would have tried to get him help, or if they'd put a bullet through his head.

"Understandable." Firmly dismissing the shitload of troubles that were waiting for them, he trailed his fingers down the line of her jaw. "Can I come in?"

She hesitated, her cheeks flushing as the air scented with the spice of her arousal.

"Yeah," she at last conceded.

"Good."

Cammy stepped back to give him room to enter, only to gasp in surprise when he abruptly scooped her off her feet. Kicking the door shut with his foot, he cradled her against his chest as he headed toward the back of the small, cozy home.

"Ice," she said with a halfhearted protest.

He glanced down, his inner cat already anticipating her sweet taste. The only question was whether to lick her from head to toe…or to start at the bottom and work his way up.

"You said I could come in," he reminded her, his voice a low growl.

She glared at him even as her eyes heated with sensual anticipation. "I didn't say you could manhandle me."

"I've been waiting to manhandle you for a very long time."

He moved through the open door, entering the bedroom that was filled with a four-poster bed with a pretty quilt, and a hand-carved rocker in the corner.

Holding her heated gaze, Ice lowered her onto the wide mattress. Her entire body quivered, as if silently urging him to pounce. To conquer. To take what he had ached to possess since he had caught a glimpse of her. But he brutally fought back the primitive instincts of his animal.

Stark, panting lust had its place, but not now.

Not with Cammy.

She was not just a sexy female who stimulated his senses. She was the enthralling, maddening creature who was now a vital part of his existence.

Placing his knee on the edge of the bed, Ice leaned down to brush his mouth over hers. It was a mere whisper of a touch, but it was enough to send a jolt of searing heat through his body.

Her hair spilled over the quilt, her lips curving with a sinful smile. "Ward was right about one thing," she murmured.

Reaching down, Ice grabbed the bottom of his sweatshirt to tug it over his head.

"What's that?" he demanded, tossing the shirt onto the floor.

"You are a savage."

He chuckled, straightening so he could wrench off his boots and then slide his jeans down his legs. Kicking them aside, he crawled onto the bed, sinking into the soft mattress.

"Oh, I intend to be a lot more savage before this night's over," he assured her, stretching beside her trembling body.

She reached up, her fingers gently tracing the tattoo of a sleeping puma that was inked onto his upper chest.

"Is that a warning or a promise?"

With a groan he feathered kisses over her cheeks, a quiver shaking his body. Did she know exactly where this night was leading?

He did.

Before he left the bed, he fully intended to claim her.

The sort of "together forever and ever" claiming.

Anticipation shivered through him. With every kiss it became more and more difficult to leash the need to be buried deep in the sweet heat of her body.

"Both," he muttered as he moved to trace his lips along the stubborn line of her jaw. She tasted just as delicious as he'd anticipated. Decadent. Intoxicating. Sweet sin.

Dear Goddess, he would never have enough of her.

She gave a small gasp of pleasure. "Shouldn't we talk first?"

Sweeping his tongue along the curve of her ear he returned to claim her lips in a kiss of sheer possession.

"Talk about what?"

Beneath him Cammy stirred, her hands grasping his shoulders. "Us."

"What's there to talk about?" he demanded, his fingers stroking down the length of her throat. "You belong to me."

Her fingers curled against his chest. The hint of claws digging into his flesh made Ice shudder with pleasure. Inside, his cat purred with anticipation.

The animal liked claws and fangs during sex.

"Your arrogant ass is showing again."

With a chuckle, he studied the hectic color that stained her cheeks. "Do you want to touch it?" he asked, his gaze lowering to the plush softness of her lips "I promise to pet yours if you want."

She gave a sudden laugh, her mischievous cat glinting in her eyes.

"How did I ever think you didn't know how to enjoy life?" she whispered.

His cock twitched. She was always beautiful. But when she smiled she became irresistible.

Swooping his head lower, he dipped his tongue

into the moist heat of her mouth. Raw desire sparked between them, the heat nearly combustible as he reached down to tug at the belt that held her robe together.

His breath lodged in his throat as her tongue tangled with his own. This female had always been capable of making him forget everything. His duty. His family. Hell, he was lucky if he could remember what day it was.

All he could think about was claiming her as his own.

Lifting his head, he studied her with a fierce gaze. "I didn't fully enjoy life."

Her smile faded, her fingers skimming over his chest in an unconsciously soothing motion. "What do you mean?"

He held her gaze as he gently separated the robe to expose the ivory loveliness of her soft curves.

"Earlier you asked me if I was lonely and I said no," he murmured, leaning down to brush his lips along the upper curve of her breast. "That wasn't entirely true, but by concentrating on my duty I could pretend I had a purpose."

She gave a choked groan, her fingers tangling in his hair. "And now?"

He slowly explored her bountiful flesh, relishing the intoxicating smell of her arousal perfuming the air.

"Now I've realized there's much more than duty."

"Hmm." She arched her back as he lashed his tongue over the tip of her hardened nipple. "Very enlightened."

Savage desire pulsed through him, his cat

brushing against his skin with the need to savor the heat of her desire. He suckled her nipple before using the edge of his teeth to pleasure her.

"Do you want me to tell you about the things I've discovered I enjoy?" he asked, his lips pressing a trail of kisses to her other breast.

She gave a low groan, restlessly stirring against the quilt. "I think already knew that you enjoyed this," she choked out.

Ice grasped her hips, holding her still as he kissed the underside of her breast before heading downward. He intended to make a banquet of her, tasting and biting until she was screaming with the force of her orgasm.

"I didn't know that my day could be brightened by the sight of a particular female," he murmured, scraping the tips of his elongated fangs against the tender flesh of her stomach. "Or that her smile could make my heart miss a beat." He slid his hands beneath her legs, tugging them apart so he could settle between them. "Or her scent send my cat into a frenzy of need."

She shivered as she tilted her head to watch him with glowing eyes. "You aren't the only one frenzied."

With a chuckle he turned his head to nuzzle the soft skin of her inner thigh. "Good. But it's more than that."

"Is it?" she breathed, clearly struggling to concentrate as his lips skimmed toward the sweet center of her pleasure.

"Yeah." He sucked in a deep breath of her intoxicating musk. Hunger blasted through his body even as he fiercely leashed his need. "Suddenly I want to share dinner with the pack just to watch you with your friends. And I'm starting to plan the house I intend for us to share."

"Share?" Her fingers clenched in his hair as his tongue lapped through her moist heat.

"With a lush garden where our cubs can play," he continued.

Her eyes widened, but before she could respond he grasped her hips, tilting her to the perfect angle. Then, settling on the mattress, he lapped at her cream.

"Ice," she breathed, arching beneath his relentless onslaught.

Ice savored her sweetness, dipping his tongue into her sweet little channel. "Tell me that you're mine."

She made a strangled sound of pleasure as he stroked back to the top of her clit. Reaching down she tangled her fingers in his hair. "We can talk later."

He chuckled, finding her tiny bundle of pleasure to suck between his lips. When her hips bucked off the mattress, he lifted his head to meet her smoldering gaze. "Say the words."

She groaned, roughly tugging at his hair. "Later."

He could scent her nearing climax, his cock twitching in reaction. "Now," he growled.

"I'm yours," she breathed.

He continued to taste her luscious cream. "Again."

Her grip on his hair eased, her fingers gently touching his face as if sensing the importance of this moment.

"I'm yours, Ice," she murmured with a blunt simplicity that soothed his inner doubts.

"And Rage?" It was impossible to halt the question.

She grimaced. "I told myself it was easier to seek a male who was more a friend than an alpha. I thought my cat was too dominant to accept a mate who challenged me." She traced the curve of his lips, her face softening with an emotion he never dared to hope he would witness. "But thank the Goddess, I was wrong. What I need is you. Just you, Ice."

"Yes."

Joy rushed through him as he bent his head, intending to taste her climax on his tongue. Cammy, however, surged upward to grab his shoulders.

"Wait, Ice."

He froze, his cat on instant alert. Had he done something wrong? Had she changed her mind? "What?"

Her eyes blazed a hunger that matched his own. "I want you inside me when I come."

A growl rumbled deep in his chest even as raw relief shuddered through him.

"Yes." With a last, lingering lap of his tongue, Ice surged upward, claiming her mouth in a kiss of stark possession.

For years he'd fantasized about having this female in his arms. In his bed.

Now he was so desperate to make love to her, he wasn't sure he could leash his cat. He was quivering with the need to impale her with his aching cock, pounding them both to a swift, explosive orgasm, but he was acutely aware that this was their first time together.

Didn't females like it soft and romantic?

"Tell me if I'm too rough," he murmured, settling on top of her.

"I'm a Hunter, darling." She dug her claws into his shoulders, her legs wrapped instinctively around his waist in a silent offering. "There's nothing you can give me that I can't take."

A rough groan was wrenched from Ice's throat at her husky challenge. "Then hold on, kitty."

Holding her bold gaze, he breached her entrance with the head of his cock, hesitating to savor the feel of her moist flesh wrapped around his crown.

His breath hissed between his teeth. Nothing had ever felt so good.

Beneath him Cammy squirmed, the musk of her puma scenting the air. "No more playing," she muttered. "I need you inside me."

"You're mine," he murmured. "My mate." He pressed an inch of his broad erection inside her. "My partner." Another inch slid into her slick heat. "My love."

"Forever," she added, sinking her teeth into the spot where his neck met his shoulder.

The pleasure-pain jolted through him, and with one fierce thrust he had his cock buried deep inside her. They groaned together in raw pleasure. This was what he wanted. Why he'd chosen his warrior female.

It was two Pantera mating on their most primitive level, the pounding of their hearts and the press of their cats just beneath their skin.

Tilting his head down, he covered her lips in a searing kiss, the pleasure shockingly intense.

"How have I survived without you?" he muttered as he began to move. She gave a groan of appreciation, her hips lifting off the mattress in silent invitation. "You complete me."

"Ice," she breathed. "My mate."

Pressing his face into the curve of her neck, he pistoned in and out of her heat, keeping a ruthless pace. A part of him wanted to make this last, but his cat refused to be denied. On some level he'd been searching for this female his entire life. Now it was time to claim her.

Releasing his claws, he allowed them to score through the skin along her lower back. The shallow wounds would heal, leaving behind four silvery scars that were a pagan mark of ownership.

Heady bliss swirled through him, intensified by the feel of her pussy clenched tight around his cock. He would never have enough of her. Never. Ever.

Hearing the fractured sound of her breath, he intensified the force of his thrusts, the bed banging against the wall as they moved together in a savage rhythm.

Still, it wasn't until he felt her orgasm squeezing his cock that he sought his own release. Giving one last surge, he buried himself until his balls were flush against her ass and allowed his climax to shatter him into a million pieces of sated joy.

Nothing had prepared him for the erotic ferocity of making love to his mate. It felt as if the world had just tilted on its axis, leaving them in a new, wonderful place.

Raising his head, he studied his female's stunned

expression. Clearly he wasn't the only one reeling from the intensity of their mating.

It was Cammy, however, who at last broke the thick silence.

"So tell me about this house you intend to build for me and my cubs."

REAUX

LAURA WRIGHT

CHAPTER 1

"Are you comfortable?"

Karen stared straight ahead as she sat on the edge of the couch in the Healer's office. Was she comfortable? What a strange, impossible idea. She hadn't known comfort for a very long time. Maybe since the night before she was taken. Maybe when she was tucked in around her family dinner table twelve years ago, having...what was it again? Spaghetti? No. Her mom didn't make good red sauce. Tacos? No.

A soft smile touched her lips. Chicken and dumplings. Her mother made the absolute best.

A rush of pain echoed through her. She missed that wonderful woman...even more now that she had passed. Never to see her grandchildren. Caleb. Or Ward. Or...

"Let's talk about your offspring," the female Healer said, trying once again to pull Karen back into her universe.

"Children," Karen corrected woodenly.

"Of course."

"I have three."

"Yes, I know."

Caleb, Ward...and the one she'd known for seconds only...before he was ripped from her arms, before they'd injected her with drugs to force her to sleep. And forget. As if that was even a possibility. No amount of drugs could steal the memory of birth, or the squalling face of an infant. She'd named him Tate. After her grandfather. Who knew what he called himself now. If he was called anything. If he was even alive.

Her chest tightened to the point of pain, but she didn't flinch. It was a pain that was familiar now. One she'd learned to live with. One that had strangely come to feel good.

Right.

"I think we should talk about them, Karen," the female said in a gentle voice. "Each one. Let's start with Caleb."

That sweet three-year-old face appeared in her mind. Her baby Caleb, who was hardly a baby anymore thanks to his Pantera blood. The Healers were worried about Caleb. Actually, what they were worried about was Karen's ability to care for him. After she'd been brought back to the Wildlands a few days ago...after she'd been abducted by Ward, by her son, who'd been told she hadn't wanted him—she'd pretty much fallen apart. Quietly, gently, unquestioningly, apart. Jean-Baptiste and one of the Healers she worked with had found her in the living room of her little house, holding Caleb and refusing to let him go.

She'd been holding him for seven hours straight.

"Caleb," the female pressed. "Tell me how he's reacted to being here. In the Wildlands."

Karen, of course, had agreed to start therapy. She'd been told that this female Healer, Mackenzie, was one of the best. Sharp, insightful, probing.

Clinical.

"Would you agree that after being born in captivity, growing up in captivity, Caleb needs as much normalcy as possible?" the Healer probed.

Despite the weirdness of his mother's seven-hour hug, Caleb was great. Happier than she'd ever seen him. Living in the Wildlands had been the best thing for him. The air, the magic. His Pantera side was being fulfilled every day. He loved being with the older males, learning about who he was…

Caleb was great.

Pain rippled through her bones and she bit her lip. What about Ward? Didn't anyone care about Ward? Where was he? Was he still alive? Was he hurting?

And Tate?

On an exhale, she put her head in her hands.

"Is the wound hurting you?" Mackenzie asked, referring to the bullet that had grazed the flesh of her temple when she, Ice and Cammy had escaped yet another of Benson Enterprises' horrifying labs.

"No," Karen whispered into her palms. The wound that pained her was deep and far reaching. It was a wound that would never heal until she knew her children were safe.

"Tell me what Ward said to you when he held you captive."

You didn't want me.

"Did he hurt you?" the female pressed.

No. I did the hurting.

And in the end, Ward had helped her. Had sacrificed himself for her. Her child, her cub, as the Pantera called them, who was now a grown man. Despite being chronologically nine, he nearly looked and acted as old as she.

There was a sigh from behind the desk. Poor, annoyed Healer.

"Karen, maybe it would be a good idea if, while you receive treatment, Caleb is placed with one of our families."

Startled, Karen glanced up. "What?"

The female's eyes flashed. She'd gained Karen's attention. Finally. The chess move made Karen not only dislike the female, but distrust her.

"Just for a short time. We have some wonderful families. Even perhaps with our leader, Raphael, and his mate. They have a young cub. I'm sure he would enjoy—"

"You're not taking my child." The tone that came out of Karen wasn't normal for someone with zero Pantera blood. It was lethal.

"Please don't be angry," Mackenzie told her in an irritatingly gentle voice. "Think of Caleb. His needs…"

Heat rushed up from Karen's neck into her head, making her dizzy. Her hands were balled into fists, and she knew if she didn't get out of there, she was going to do something stupid. Something that could make things worse for her and Caleb.

"I don't feel very well," she muttered, coming to her feet. Her legs felt unsteady, like they were filled with water. "We'll do this another time. I need to go home and lie down."

"Can I help you?"

"No."

Mackenzie called after her, but Karen heard nothing as she stumbled out of the room and closed the door. She never wanted to see that female again. She'd go to Raphael herself. After all that she and the other rats had been through... Taking away what was most important to them...

Her child...

Can you blame them? You're falling apart. It felt like that. Something had unleashed itself in that cell Ward had put her in. Something panicky and wild. Maybe she should take Caleb and go. But where? And would the Pantera let her take one of their own out of the Wildlands? Especially now, when they were calling back all of their kind?

The idea of Caleb being taken... Like Ward and Tate. Suddenly, she couldn't breathe. She grabbed hold of the back of a chair in the empty waiting room. The dark waiting room. Or was that her vision?

No light.

No air.

Crying out, she pushed away from the chair and stumbled forward. The world was listing, like she was out to sea. Heat surged into her skull. She grabbed the first thing she could find. Door handle. She turned and pushed. Where was the cool air? She wanted out. But all that met her was warm, hard, solid. Her legs buckled.

"Hey. Hey." A male voice entered her consciousness. Low timbre. Concerned.

And then she was being lifted or carried or

helped. Eased down. When her back felt the steady support of the wall, she sagged against it and released a breath.

"Are you a patient of Mackenzie's?" the male asked.

No. No more Mackenzie.

She must've shaken her head because he asked, "Dante? Suja?"

His voice, it was like a drug. The kind that instantly soothed, made you want to cleave to it, curl up against it.

"You're all right," he assured her. "Can you look at me? Talk to me?"

She felt her chin being lifted, and she opened her eyes. Blinking a few times, the world came back into focus. A room, office, but not like Mackenzie's. This was like…nature inside.

"What's your name?"

She turned to the man. No…to the *male* who was crouched before her. Like the Pantera cat he no doubt hid inside him. His black hair was closely shaved to his skull, and his face was starkly, brutally handsome, all sharp angles with a heavy mouth. But his gray eyes were the kindest, most sincere she'd ever seen.

He reached for her, his hand coming to her cheek. "Breathe, female," he said as he stroked her skin. "In and out."

Hypnotized, she stared at him. She knew many of the Healers. But this one…this gorgeous, gentle, yet no doubt deadly creature was a stranger to her.

"My name is Reaux. Do you want to tell me who you are?"

His voice...whatever properties it contained, was a balm to her wounds. It cocooned her. Made her feel safe. Understood. Cared for. It made her feel like she could finally trust—

Tears broke from her eyes and she started to cry. Deep, heaving sobs that had refused to come for days, weeks, years. They weren't the kind that stemmed from fear or agony—those had dried up long ago—but the kind that came from intense release.

She couldn't stop.

She didn't want to.

And when the magical creature called Reaux pulled her into his arms, and held her close, she let the downpour come.

***

He was an idiot.

A reckless male.

Holding this female. Stroking her cheek.

But he couldn't let her go. Steady tears, her heart bleeding in front of him, her fingers wrapped tightly around his shirt sleeves? This was what he'd wanted from the first moment he'd been confirmed as a Healer. To clear the pain, to define the ache.

To heal the heart and mind.

As her grip on him tightened, his lip curled. Mistakes like him—curses of the blood—they didn't get to see their dreams or their desires realized. They were happy with what they got. And speaking of desire, he mused darkly, he needed to detach this female from his body and send her on her way before wet eyes turned into a wet sex. She might be human, no doubt one of the rats who'd been rescued and brought to the Wildlands, but she would still very much be affected by him.

That was the last thing he wanted—to have his colleagues think he'd allowed a single, female patient near him.

He eased her back, hoping it wasn't already too late. He'd been incredibly reckless. Hoping that when he looked into her eyes, he wouldn't see that customary stain of arousal. But he was lucky for once. Beautiful light brown, almost amber orbs stared up at him. Tear-heavy to be sure, but clear. He breathed a sigh of relief.

"I'm sorry," she said, wiping her eyes.

Goddess, don't apologize, female. Not for your tears or for clinging to me like your very breath depends upon it. You have no idea how it feels. How long it's been since a female's touched me for anything other than their own sexual pleasure.

"No need to apologize," he said finally, his gaze moving over her pale, exquisite face, and the heavy fall of copper hair that framed it. "Not for your pained heart, your tears or that you needed another's strength for a moment."

Even as he said the words, his mind was telling him to disentangle himself from her, leave the office and go find one of the other emotional Healers to take over. It was only a matter of time. No doubt his body had already released the scent. Its venom, he called it now. And this female wouldn't be able to help herself. Instead of clinging to him, she'd claw him. Instead of tears, there would be cries to be touched and demands for release. Her mouth would call to his, and her hands would find his zipper.

Slowly, gently, he pulled back and stood. She made a sound like it pained her to be separated from him, and he cursed inwardly. It was happening already. Normally, he didn't get worked up when the females did. The cachet of being desperately desired had worn off. Because it had nothing to do with him, as a male. But this woman...there was something about her that interested him, drew him.

Foolish male.

As he helped her to her feet, he refused to look at her. In those eyes, at that mouth. Even now, his fingers itched to touch her hair. Just one slow drag up to her scalp.

"What's your name?" he commanded.

"Karen."

He opened the door to his office and stood before it. "You need to go, Karen. Back to where you came from."

No doubt his sharp tone shocked her. After all, he'd been kind and gentle only seconds before. But she didn't recoil from him at all.

"I was in with Mackenzie," she started. "But—"

"You should return to her. She's an excellent therapist."

She shook her head. "Not for me. She's not right. I couldn't open up to her at all. She doesn't make me feel…" She nibbled on her bottom lip.

Right. He was too late. His venom had already entered her bloodstream. "No. I'm sure she doesn't."

"You're a Healer, aren't you?"

"I treat couples only."

She didn't move from her spot near the door. "I know this is going to sound crazy. But I'm sure you've had a lot of crazy in here, right?"

"Karen, you need—"

"I think it's you, Reaux."

It was impossible to stop. His gaze slid to hers and he demanded, "What's me?"

Her expression was alive with hunger and passion. "The one. The person who can help me."

Reaux shook his head. "I'm sorry, Karen, I can't—"

"I understand that you specialize in couples, but maybe you can make an exception? Just this once."

"No."

"You don't understand."

"Trust me, I do. Now, let me take you back to Mackenzie. She may not be the perfect person to help you, but she's available."

No doubt he looked as resolute, as cold, as he sounded. But truly, it was for her own good. She only thought she wanted him, needed him. But it was the curse.

"I understand." She gave him a tight, forced smile. "Thanks for the help, but I'll find my own way."

He was used to anger from females now. But on her, it felt...wrong. "Again, I'm sorry."

"Goodbye, Reaux."

His name on her lips—those lips—was painfully tempting to hear. But he wouldn't stop her. He was many things: a mistake, a slut, a predator. But the one he was most proud of, the Healer part of him, would never intentionally hurt another soul. No matter how beautiful or how intriguing that soul was.

CHAPTER 2

"What do you mean he wouldn't help you?" Indy asked, plopping into the chair opposite Karen's desk at the clinic. "Such an asshole."

"The thing is, I don't think he is." Her body still trembling from both the session with Mackenzie and whatever that was with Reaux, Karen had come back to her office. She didn't want to go home. Didn't want anyone thinking she was falling apart again, even though she absolutely was. But with the female Healer's suggestion of taking Caleb away from her hanging over her head, she couldn't let anyone think she had fissured. Even the woman in front of her.

"Refusing to help one of us?" Indy went on, her biker chick/pixie-doll face a mask of disgust. "After all we've been through—and shit, after all *you've* been through."

She gave the woman a nod of solidarity. Indy had been her friend in captivity. A good, real friend. They understood each other, shared the pain of those times. In truth, she was the only person Karen could talk to right now who might be able to help her. Well, the only person who would talk back.

"I'd go to Raphael," Indy said, her dark blue eyes flashing.

"No." Just the idea of running to the leader of the Pantera with her complaints, putting herself and what she was struggling with on his radar… No way. "It'll be fine. I'll be fine." She shook her head. "It just seemed like he…I don't know…he understood, or something. The way he looked at me with those eyes, touched me."

"I'm sorry, what? He touched you?"

"I was really upset, crying—"

Indy's eyes bulged further. "You were crying? I've never seen you cry."

"When he held me." She forged onward. "I felt…"

"Safe?" Indy finished for her.

Karen gasped softly. "Yes. But is that even possible for us?"

"Angel makes me feel it." Her cheeks went pink as she spoke of her Healer mate. "All the time."

Karen's eyes dropped to the desk before her. Her heart actually hurt at Indy's words. Not because she begrudged her friend the obvious deep connection she had with her mate. But because with that first taste of such a connection, Karen had been denied.

"He made you feel that, Karen?" Indy asked her. "Safe?"

She looked up. Nodded.

A gentle smile touched Indy's mouth. "Then you need to go to Raphael. Hell, I'll talk with Angel. They're both Healers. I'm sure he knows him." She snorted with attitude. "Won't treat you. Couples only. Whatever."

"Are you guys talking about Reaux?"

Both women turned to the door. A very pretty female with shoulder-length blond hair and a cupid-bow mouth stood there. Her name was Gail and she was one of Jean-Baptiste's assistants. She was also a huge gossip.

"Sorry," she said with an impish shrug. "Couldn't help overhearing."

"Yeah right," Indy muttered under her breath.

"Everyone knows Reaux." A slow smile crossed the female's expression. "Or they'd like to. He's got…that thing. Can't take your eyes off him, or your hands, kind of thing. But he's impossible to catch, if you know what I mean."

Karen might've been falling apart emotionally, but she wasn't an idiot. Of course she knew what Gail was implying. And this little beastie inside her wondered if Gail had actually succeeded in the eyes-hands-catching department. But she didn't ask. Instead, she made shit very clear. "I'm not interested in knowing or catching him. Just being treated by him."

"Well, that's too bad, hon. Because he only works—"

"With couples, I know."

"He's not a 'lie on the couch and tell me about your childhood' kind of therapist. I'm assuming that's what you want."

"Don't assume, Gail," Indy put in. "Makes everyone asses."

"I was just informing. What he is. What he's not."

Karen was really tired all of a sudden. Way too tired for this back-and-forth nonsense with Gail. Caleb was playing with one of the hybrid cubs. Maybe she should go get him early.

But Indy was still hungry for more. "So? What kind of Healer is he then, Gail?"

The female's mouth broke into a wicked smile. "The sexual kind."

The tiny office went silent. Indy looked at Karen, who in turn was staring at Gail. Who seemed thrilled to be the one sharing such a juicy piece of news. No doubt the rest of the Pantera already had this info long ago.

"Reaux has this sort of gift-slash-curse thing," she continued. "Born with it. It's like his cat's pheromones also shed from his human skin."

"What the hell does that mean?" Indy asked.

"You know how your mate—Angel, right? When he's in his cat form he has a musk you can't resist?"

Indy turned bright red.

"Oh, honey, every male cat produces that. Don't be embarrassed."

"I'm not," she ground out. "Go on."

"Well, Reaux has that all the time. Cat form. Male form. He's sexually irresistible to unmated females."

Mouth open, Karen looked over at Indy, who seemed as stunned as she was.

"That's why he only works with couples," Gail said, hugging her files to her chest. "The males have marked their females, and will fight to the death for them if pushed. And most of the time the mated females are not tempted by him, anyway. He brings on a boost of sexual energy and healing to the couples. It's pretty amazing." Gail cocked her head, her cheeks flushing. "We all try and get with him. Just for a night. I hear the musk alone can send a female over the edge, if you know what I'm saying."

Yes. Yes, yes, yes. Karen understood what the female was saying. Not that it was easy to believe.

"I don't care about his musk," she said, though she'd be lying if she didn't admit she was intrigued. "I'm not looking for a combustible night with him—"

"Sweetie, you won't be able to stop yourself from wanting it. Not if you're within a few feet. But good luck if you try." And with a wink, she left the doorway and headed off down the hall.

Indy snorted. "Can you believe that shit?"

"No." She stood, legs still unsteady. She didn't know what to make of any of it. "I'm going home. I'm really tired."

"Sure. Call me if you need me, okay?"

She gave her friend a quick hug, then left the office. Now she understood. He'd thought she was reacting to his musk. She had to convince him that wasn't true. Because it didn't matter what scent he was throwing off, or who he didn't treat. She needed him. With a little kindness and care, he'd broken down something inside her. Maybe, just maybe, he could help her rebuild it. Twice as strong. So that she could hold on to the child she had, find the two she'd lost, and ultimately be the mother each deserved.

***

Shirt off, sweat glistening on his skin, Reaux lay perfectly balanced on his back on a tree branch, under the late afternoon sun and overlooking the rushing bayou. He was exhausted. Quinton and Via's session had been in the water today. There was no other way to get them out of their cats and into their human forms. They'd been stuck that way for a month. Too much damn rutting. Not to mention the constant need to remain on guard.

No longer were the enemies of the Pantera residing outside the borders of the Wildlands. More and more, they were breaching and coming to either take or destroy. Reaux had refused to visit either the flames of the bombed Headquarters or the start of the rebuild. Anger was always something to be feared with him. It seemed to intensify his musk. And with so many females around, he didn't want the attention to be taken off what was vitally important. Seemed he was retreating deeper and deeper lately.

Just as he was nodding off, the sun penetrating his skin, the scent of sweet mint rushed his nostrils. Immediately, his weary body stirred. In both defense and in awareness. His jaw tightened and his nostrils flared. What the hell was she doing here?

"Stay where you are," he growled low and fierce. "Not another step."

The sound of footfall ceased, then a weary voice responded, "Okay."

It bothered him, that thread of emotional and physical exhaustion in her tone. Made his awareness vibrate. Made everything inside him ache to help. It was why, long ago as a young cub, he'd hoped to become a Healer. Finding the reasons behind pain and working with the individual to push through it. It's what his own Healer had done for him back when his curse emerged. That, and made him feel like less of a freak.

"Why are you here, Karen?" he demanded.

"I need to talk to you."

"I told you—"

"That you only treat couples. I know."

"If you know, then you should be back at the clinic with another Healer."

"I also understand why you work with couples."

He sat up, turned to face her. "You do?"

She nodded. Standing several feet below him, surrounded in green foliage and dappled sunlight, her red hair piled on top of her head in a messy bun, she looked disturbingly pretty. She'd changed clothes and was wearing dark gray jeans and a white tank top. She had a lush, very female body; tall, strong, with incredible curves. She was human, true. But she was built for a Pantera male. To both ride and be ridden.

That thought had Reaux snarling at himself. The last thing he needed to do was have physical opinions about this woman. "You need to go, Karen. Now."

She shook her head. "No."

She was stubborn as hell. "If you understand about me, then you know you shouldn't be here. Shouldn't be anywhere near me. And why I absolutely can't treat you."

"But—"

"No buts."

"I'm not sexually interested in you, Reaux."

He stilled, his ass digging into the branch. What had she just said? He stared down at her. At first, curious. Perhaps even hopeful. Then, disbelieving.

She took a step forward despite his warning. "I'm serious."

He snorted.

"There's no desire here."

"Impossible."

"Wow."

He sighed. "I don't mean that in an arrogant way, I assure you. It's fact. A lifetime of it."

"That may be," she said, hands going to her hips. "But it has no effect on me. You have no effect on me. Maybe it's because I'm human."

He jumped down from the tree branch, landing a few feet in front of her. He was surprised and intrigued when she didn't startle. Especially when she lifted her chin at him.

"It doesn't matter what blood courses through your veins, Karen. Or any female's, for that matter. What I have inside me will turn any blood to fire." *My curse. Or as the female who gave me life used to call it, my wickedness.*

But Karen wasn't moved. "Not me. I feel zero urge to kiss you or rip your clothes off or beg you to…" She stopped, shook her head. "Look, my need for you has nothing to do with a sexual one."

Reaux stared hard into her eyes. Those pale brown pools of passion and sincerity. Impossible. He moved closer until he was only an inch or two away. He looked her over. Sniffed the air. Waited. Watched. But she didn't move. Just looked up at him with those eyes…

Impossible.

His brows drew together as he calculated what he was witnessing. The only thing he scented was sweet mint. There was not even the faintest whiff of female lust. How was such a thing... He stared hard at her. "No."

Her eyes narrowed. "You still refuse me?"

He didn't tell her that his 'no' had meant only a disbelief in her impassivity, not a refusal. "I wouldn't be the best choice for you, Karen. My training has been limited—"

"I don't care."

"You should. It's your health."

"I'm not just fighting for myself here. My son needs me to be whole or—" Her voice broke and she cursed. "Listen, I'm just asking you to try."

She had a child. And she was most definitely human. No doubt she'd had him in captivity. His gaze moved over her face.

"I need you, Reaux," she whispered. "You have no idea how much."

The deep ache that moved through him at her words was impossible to turn from. He wanted to help her. He wanted to protect her. But he also wanted to hold her again. Feel her weight against his chest, her hands through the fabric of his shirt. What was that? Not something a Healer should be feeling for his patient. How could he know? His need for a female had never been allowed to start, much less grow. It had always just been...taken.

"So," she asked softly. "What do you think?"

What did he think? This was going to be a

mistake? But that he was also incredibly curious? That he needed to help her? That perhaps he was standing in front of the one female in the world he desired, but who didn't desire him?

With a growl, he turned around and climbed back up the tree. Only when he was lying down again did he utter the words, "Come by my office tomorrow at ten."

CHAPTER 3

Karen watched him sleep in the light of the moon. The beautiful boy who was growing far too quickly, despite the deceleration of being in the Wildlands. Caleb looked so much like his older brother, Ward. Did Tate also look like them? Like her?

"Kar?"

She heard the call from the living room and eased the covers up to Caleb's chin before leaving him to dream. Out in her small living room, her friend Adrian was sitting on the couch, furiously tapping away on the keyboard of his laptop. The male was a full Pantera, but had been in the labs with her and the rats. He'd already been there a year before she'd arrived. They'd been neighbors. Cell next door. On more than one occasion, the guards had put them together to see if they would mate naturally. While the bastards watched, of course. But Adrian never touched her. And he'd been beaten for it. Over the years, they'd become friends, understood each other, protected each other. Incredibly gifted with computers, he now worked with the Geeks.

"I've checked birth records in New York for that

day and time," he said. "Nothing. I'm sure whoever took him didn't use that exact date anyway."

Karen knew it was unlikely the information would be there. Babies like Tate were being bred for experimentation. They weren't going to have birth certificates, or be adopted through state agencies. But she had to try.

"I'm going to research adoptions around then," he added. "I'll follow up with doctors. Schools."

She came over to the couch and sat down beside him. "Thank you so much for doing this."

"It helps me too, if that makes sense."

"It does."

"Sometimes I wish…" He trailed off.

"What?"

"I don't know. That I'd…you and me had…instead of what they did to you." He heaved a sigh, gave her a half smile. "If they'd have been mine, maybe something would've been different for you. At least I could've helped with the cubs."

His words seared into her. They were lovely and generous. But they were fantasy. "They wouldn't have let you anywhere near the babies when they were born, Adrian. They would've known how you'd react if they'd tried to take your child away."

"Then I could have helped you," he said.

"You are." She put a hand on his shoulder. "Right now."

His eyes shuttered, but he nodded. "We'll find them, Karen. As long as it takes, okay?"

"Okay." It was everything. Keeping Caleb with her, and finding Ward and Tate. And she so appreciated her friend's generosity. "But not tonight," she said pointedly. "One more hour, max. Then you're out of here. I know you have a date."

Adrian's muscles flexed at the mention of the Hunter he was seeing. Like many of the Pantera males who'd come back from the labs, he had a difficult time opening up to anyone, much less the females. It was like his body was on constant alert. He wanted to relax and enjoy himself, but it never felt…safe.

A knock at the door brought Karen out of her thoughts. She gave Adrian a look. "Is Alisa meeting you here?"

"No."

She got up and headed for the door, the nerves in her belly fraying. Like Adrian, she had that constant state of alert thing too. Came from being held captive. You never knew what or who was coming for you.

She pulled back the door and was surprised to see Reaux standing there. Moonlight at his back.

"Hello, Karen."

Casually dressed in a black T-shirt and jeans, he held a file in his hand. Her heart stuttered at the sight of him.

"I thought our appointment was tomorrow," she said, concerned about the stuttering. She'd made it very clear to him that she wasn't affected by his musk. "In your office?"

"It is. I brought something for you to fill out. A few questions that are better answered without time constraints or pressure."

"Oh, okay." She took the file, though she thought it was kind of odd that he'd bring it by in person, and at night. But she wasn't about to question it. She needed him. "Thank you."

"Of course."

She waited for him to turn around and head out, but when he didn't, she asked, "Was there something else?"

His nostrils flared slightly, and his brow furrowed.

"Reaux? What's going on?" She prayed he wasn't having second thoughts. Again.

"Kar, I think I might have found something." Adrian took that exact moment to pull up alongside her at the door. When he noticed Reaux standing there, he acknowledged him with a tip of the chin. "Hey there."

Reaux didn't say anything. But he was sure staring, the muscles in his neck bulging slightly.

"Adrian," Karen said quickly, trying to figure out what was happening in her foyer. Or maybe she was trying to avoid it. "This is Reaux. The Healer I was telling you about."

"Oh." As if that made all the difference, he stuck out his hand. "Good to meet you. Thanks for helping out my girl here."

Reaux looked like he might shift. Right then and there. And she'd seen enough Pantera males in the lab—pissed-off males—to know when a shift was coming. There was this electricity in the air, and the features on the male changed slightly. To more feline. The deadly, predator kind of feline.

But instead, he said coolly, "I understand now. I'll see you tomorrow." Before turning and stalking away.

***

As rain pelted the Wildlands, Reaux addressed the two males seated across from him. "I don't want to hear about her history from either of you." He'd built a covered deck off the back of his office at the clinic. It had proved useful, both for himself and for the couples he worked with. Or now, for a quick breakfast meeting with the Pantera leader and the Healer.

"I was only going to give you certain pieces of the puzzle," Jean-Baptiste said in between bites of apple, the new tattoo he'd just had done of his mate's eyes flashing on the back of his hand. "What most would know. Nothing intimate."

"She has a cub," Raphael put in. The leader of the Pantera, who also happened to be Reaux's cousin, was dressed casually in jeans and a black sweatshirt. No doubt relishing a day without suit and tie. "His name's Caleb."

Reaux shook his head. Of course he knew the woman had a child, but as he'd told the males several times already, he wanted to hear from Karen herself.

"Backstory on my new patient aside," he said to Raphael, pointedly, "isn't there something you want to say to me?"

The male's gold eyes flashed. "You called us here, Reaux."

"Aren't you concerned?"

"About what?"

"How my curse could affect this human female? One who's obviously been through intense trauma."

Raphael snorted. "Cousin, I've never been

worried. That was your mother's, and my aunt's, irrational issue. One she seemed to relish torturing you about. You've always been smart about what you think you can handle. I don't need to be involved." He released a weary breath. "Besides, I have a few other pressing matters to deal with."

"Like the safety of our species," Jean-Baptiste put in.

"Shit…not just safety anymore. The survival."

Reaux tensed, almost into fighting mode. "What's happened?" First and foremost, he was Pantera. Ready to battle, protect. Ready to use his teeth and claws on anything that threatened his kind. "Has there been another suicide bombing?"

"No," Raphael admitted. "But we know the reason behind it. Trying to destroy information on a biological virus Christopher developed that could wipe out the Pantera. He didn't want us to know it existed at all."

The cat inside Reaux pawed and snarled to get out. "How the hell could he create such a thing?"

"He had our kind to play with and experiment on for a long time, Reaux," JB said, the metal in his lip and eyebrow flashing as a quick burst of lightning flickered in the sky. "I fear he knows our DNA better than we do."

This bastard needed to be put down. "Was the research destroyed?"

"Looks like it," Raphael said. "But we'll have confirmation soon. I'm hoping something can be salvaged. If we can get our hands on the formula, we can create an antidote. Or that's the hope."

"Karen can tell you more about it," Jean-Baptiste said.

The woman's name made Reaux's skin tighten. "What?"

"I know you don't want backstory, but she was there. Just a few days ago. It was her son, Ward, who gave us the information. After he abducted Karen first." He shook his head. "Still don't know what to make of that. Hero or villain. But at least he got our people to safety."

"Holy shit," Reaux uttered. "That poor woman."

Raphael lifted a brow. "So. Do you really want me to say you can't help her?"

"Hell yes."

"And would you follow that order if I gave it?"

"Fuck no." The grin he shot the male was dark and half-assed.

Both Raph and Jean-Baptiste laughed. It was a difficult line to tread, leading a group of males and females who were at their core predatory animals who wished to do what they wanted—were driven by instinct to do what they wanted. But Raphael handled it well. Was fair and thoughtful in his rule.

"What's really the problem here?" Jean-Baptiste asked. "Are you attracted to her? Not that I would blame you. She's hot."

Raphael shot him the side-eye. "Don't let your female hear you talking like that."

JB snorted. "Please. It's one of our games. My mate and I. Genevieve says who she thinks is hot. I say who I think is hot. Then when we're both so jealous we're about to lose our minds, we both shift into our cats and get nast—"

Reaux cleared his throat. "Yeah, we get the picture, brother."

Jean-Baptiste chuckled darkly.

"Are you attracted to her, Reaux?" Raphael asked.

Reaux evaded the question. Mainly because he wasn't sure how he felt about the woman. How he should feel about her. "She claims to not be affected by me."

His fellow Healer, tattoo-lover, and serious oversharer nearly choked on the last bit of apple. "How's that possible?"

Reaux pointed at the male. "Exactly."

"She's not mated, is she?" Raphael asked.

"I didn't think so. But...she could be seeing someone." The words sounded like gravel in his throat. "Do either of you know a Pantera called Adrian?"

Jean-Baptiste nodded. "I checked him out when he and the others came in."

"He's a rat? Hybrid?"

"Full Pantera," JB told him. "Captured early, and held in one of the labs. Incredibly gifted with IT. I hear he was a fearless protector to the females on the inside. Or tried to be."

Hero type. Sounded like just the kind of male Karen would choose. A good male. Why, then, did Reaux want to rip out his throat?

"What does it matter who she's seeing?" Raphael asked him, his eyes humming with amusement. "You know, if you're not interested."

Reaux sent him a feral glare. "Screw you, cousin."

The leader of the Pantera laughed. And just as JB joined in, the door to Reaux's office buzzed.

"She's here." Reaux was up, out of his seat in seconds.

"Yeah, he's not into her," Jean-Baptiste uttered, shoving back his chair.

"Not at all." Raphael stood. "I suppose we can leave the way we came. Finish breakfast at home with my mate and cub."

JB nodded. "I've got to head back to work." A slow smile touched his pierced lips. "Or I could slip back into bed with Genevieve and make a second breakfast out of her—"

"Look," Reaux cut in on a growl. "Rain's stopped. Thanks for coming. Talk to you guys later."

After the two chuckling males took off, Reaux went inside his office. The first thing that hit him was the scent of sweet mint. *Damn, this is going to be a problem.* He'd have to breathe though his mouth. And then he saw her. Seated on one of the leather chairs. Her dark blue tank, jeans and sexy red hair were wet from the rain. Jaw tight, nostrils irritatingly flared, he lifted his gaze to meet hers. Did she have to be so beautiful? And Goddess, did her smile have to light up his insides like that?

The cat inside him flexed its claws, wondering if she smiled at that Geek, Adrian, in the same way.

A growl exited Reaux's throat. Thoughts like that were foolish and pointless. Though Pantera took no issue with Healer/patient relationships, as they did in the human world, Reaux was no ordinary Healer—or male, for that matter. He didn't carry on relationships. And who knew what Karen's situation was. She could very well be claimed by that—

"Good morning," he said coolly, cutting off his thoughts and taking the seat across from her.

"Thank you again," she said. "For this."

"Of course. Can I get you anything? Water? Tea?"

"No thanks. And here's the form you wanted me to fill out." After handing it to him, she glanced around. "Your office is really nice. Not like Mackenzie's. Not like anything I've seen here. It's so…calming. Like you've brought the outside in."

That was exactly what he'd wanted to do when he'd brought in the plants, had the furniture built with native wood. Put in the skylights himself. They were Pantera, after all—well, most of them—and surrounding themselves with their natural elements seemed to eliminate the anxiety most felt when they came for help.

"Where would you like to start?" he asked, trying like hell to keep himself from drowning in her scent.

She chewed her lip thoughtfully, which only managed to intrigue his cat.

"There's no wrong place, Karen," he assured her.

"Alright." She inhaled deeply, then said, "Well, I was taken from my family when I was seventeen and tossed into a cell. For the next twelve years, I was beaten, experimented on and inseminated. I gave birth three times, though I'm still a virgin. I only have one of those children today, and I'm afraid he'll get taken from me too." She lifted her chin. "I'm here today to make sure that doesn't happen."

CHAPTER 4

Karen was hardly surprised at the shock she saw on Reaux's extraordinarily handsome face. She'd pretty much laid it all out. Well, the headlines, anyway.

"Not sure where to go with that?" she asked him with a nervous laugh.

He scrubbed a hand over his chin. "How do you think I can help you keep your son?"

Good question. She wasn't exactly sure herself. "I have a lot of anger and fear and resentment built up inside me. It's part of my DNA now. It's what's holding me captive. Not the bars or those pieces of shit who stole me away from my home and family. I need to find a way to release it."

His eyes searched hers, as if the answers were somehow hidden away. And maybe they were. Maybe he could find them. Those incredibly beautiful gray orbs seemed like they held an unnatural power.

"I tend to think that emotion," he began, "good or bad, positive or negative, is energy. It's fluid. It can move in and out. Like breathing."

"You don't think emotion can get trapped sometimes?"

"You clearly believe it. Which is far more powerful than what I think."

"Reaux, I want to know what you think. That's why I'm here. To get an answer. For you to tell me the steps I need to take to release all of this...shit."

"Have you tried meditation?"

"No," she said.

"It can be very effective for calming the brain as well as the nervous system. Exercise too. And certain foods... I can put a plan in place. If these three components work, you may not even need me."

Her brown eyes narrowed. "What are you doing?"

"And if that doesn't work, there are also medications—"

"Stop." She drew back.

"What's the problem?"

"I know what you're doing."

"You wanted my advice. My counsel."

"And you're giving me a few home remedies to get me out of here," she accused hotly. "You still think I want to jump your bones!"

"I'm trying to help you, Karen. Maybe my methods—"

"This isn't help," she ground out, coming to her feet. If he wasn't going to take this seriously, then what was the point? "This is bullshit."

"There." He crossed his arms over his chest. "Right now. Tell me what's going on inside your body, your brain and your heart."

"W-what..." she stuttered, looking around for a hidden camera or something. "What is this? A game?"

But Reaux was looking at her. Hard. Intently. "Tell me. Now. What are you feeling?"

At first she wanted to tell him to go to hell. That whatever this was he was doing wouldn't work. But the way he was staring at her...those eyes. She felt...

"Heat," she uttered. "Building. Bubbling. Can't go anywhere. Can't go over. Up and down, inside my mind. There's nowhere for it to go."

She stopped talking and just stood there, eyes wide, breathing shallow.

"Sit down, Karen," he said gently. When she didn't move, he gave her an encouraging smile. "It's okay."

Tears broke in her eyes as she melted down into the chair. That was brutal. Strange. And yet, she felt perceptibly lighter.

"I'm sorry," he began. "I know it's shocking to the system, but it's the best way I've found to deal with emotional pain. Force it to the surface. See what it looks like. Feels like."

Karen didn't say anything. She couldn't. Just swiped at the tears staining her cheeks.

"Yesterday," he said, "when you cried in my arms. It was torrential." He studied her for a moment. "When was the last time—"

"Crying is a weakness," she whispered. "Can't allow it. Couldn't allow it."

"But you did. In here."

Yes. Exactly. She stood up again. Reaux's gaze followed the movement. No doubt he thought she was leaving, that maybe she regretted coming to him. But instead of walking out the door, she grabbed the front of her chair and started dragging it toward him.

"What are you doing?" he said, his tone wary.

"Coming closer."

"I see that. But why?"

When she finally landed, a good six inches before him, her knees brushing his, she said in a fraught voice, "Look, I don't understand it, but your...physical presence helps me. Changes how I breathe. Makes it okay, even healthy, for me to cry." She studied his expression for a moment. Shook her head. "It's not sexual in any way, so don't go all nuts."

"I'm not going all nuts." His tone was dark and foreboding.

"You're worried I'm going to rip your clothes off with my teeth."

His nostrils flared. "I wouldn't say worried, exactly."

"Then what?"

His eyes delved into hers. "Maybe your *mate* wouldn't be comfortable with it. How you need to be close to me."

She looked suddenly confused. "I don't have a mate."

"The male at your house last night..." he began darkly.

"Oh, Adrian." She shook her head. "No. He's a friend. A close friend. He's probably going to need some of this too. But don't worry, he wouldn't want to jump your bones either."

Reaux didn't laugh at her obvious joke. Didn't even crack a smile.

"Adrian and I understand each other," she continued. "We help each other. That's it."

"You were in the lab together?"

"Yes."

"Is he the father…"

"No," she said quickly. "I don't know who the father is, for Caleb or any of my children." She looked away for a second. At the cluster of native plants in the corner. "The one who abducted me just a few days ago, Ward, he'd been told from infancy that I never wanted him. That I'd basically tossed him aside. He clearly favors the Pantera side of himself. He's just nine in human years, but he looks almost as old as me. A man. I never got to see him grow up." Her gaze slid back to Reaux. "How do I grieve that without the anger?"

"You don't," he said simply. "But you do need to grieve it."

"He's just out there somewhere now. He was hurt, shot, trying to help us escape. Raphael has people looking for him now, and I hope and pray…" She shrugged, tears snaking down her cheeks again. What was happening to her? She was a walking tear duct around this guy. "But what about Tate, you know? My oldest. My first. He was ripped out of my arms before I could even kiss him goodbye. That's why Adrian was over last night. He's helping me try and find Tate, track him down."

"And if you can't?"

She looked up at him like he'd just punched her in the gut. "That's not the point. I have to try. I have to know. They're my babies, Reaux. I can't rest until I know they're safe."

He released a breath. "I understand. I don't mean to imply they won't be found, Karen. I'm only concerned for your emotional well-being."

"I'll deal with that." She gave him a sad smile. "I am dealing with it. But they are, and will always be, my first priority."

Reaux looked at her a long time. Then a gentle smile touched his normally hard mouth. "You're a wonderful mother."

Karen gasped softly. "How can you say that? How can you know that?"

"Because I had the opposite. My mother was always around. Always knew exactly where I was. Not out of love or care. But to censure me."

They were only a foot apart, but Karen felt herself leaning closer. "Why would she treat you like that?"

He shook his head. "Doesn't matter."

"It matters to me."

Those startling gray eyes locked with hers, and inside her ribs that muscle she'd always protected, or ignored, beat with awareness.

"This thing I was born with," he told her. "She saw it as a curse. As an embarrassment. As a sign I was wicked. And she always let me know how disgusted she was by me." He inhaled sharply. "I apologize. I shouldn't be telling you any of this."

"No, don't feel that way. I'm glad you did."

Something, for a half second at the most, glistened in those eyes of his. His cat? His emotions? The child, or cub, he'd once been? She couldn't read it. And then he pulled back and said in a cool tone, "I think we're done for the day."

Everything in her said to push him, encourage him. To be treated like that by the one person you should be able to trust above all others…it had to have cut very deep. But if anyone understood that feelings only came out when they wanted to come out, it was her.

She stood up and pushed her chair back into place. "Tomorrow?" she asked, turning to face him again. "Same time?" She tried a little smile. "Same place?"

He didn't bite. "Let me check my schedule. I'll let you know."

She tried not to show her concern, but it wasn't easy. When she went to the door, she stopped before she crossed the threshold into the reception area and glanced back. "Reaux?"

He looked up from the file he was holding. His face was a mask of impassivity. "Yes?"

"I feel a little better. Lighter. I think I released some of it today."

"I'm glad, Karen."

But he didn't look it, and she wondered, as she headed out, if she was going to hear from him again. Or if this was their one and only session.

***

After the bombing, a temporary Headquarters had been set up the garden house near Raphael and Ashe's home. It could barely contain the personnel, many of whom worked outside on makeshift tables or even up against trees. No one seemed to take issue with the close quarters. Except Reaux. He rarely went anywhere with crowds or clusters of female Pantera. It was expected of him, and a habit now. But today he needed to see a friend.

As he walked through the house, searching, he tried to keep a low profile. But it wasn't long before his scent gave him away.

"Hi, Reaux," a female called, glancing up from her desk. Which she shared with another female and a Hunter male called Night. All three of them grinned with intent and beckoned him over.

He nodded, but kept going. As he did, low growls and deep inhalations followed his every movement.

"Causing problems?" an amused male voice said the second Reaux entered a bedroom the size of a closet.

"Not trying to," Reaux answered, dropping into a chair near the male's metal desk.

Irek gave him a grin. "It's good to see you, Cursed One."

Reaux laughed. Always did. His cubhood friend had been there through it all. Seen and heard everything, and even shared his own troubles from the past. "You know I wouldn't normally come to you, but I need your help."

Irek was a spy, and had been living in Germany for the past five years. But just recently, like so many, he had been called back to the Wildlands.

"I'm wide open," the male said, his blue eyes flashing with interest.

"No you're not," Reaux countered. "I'm sure your ass is deeply entrenched in this bio weapon thing."

Dark brows lifted. "You know about that?"

"My cuz."

"Right, Raphael." He shrugged. "I am, but I can multitask. You know that."

Reaux nodded. "I do. But I'm not talking about how you regularly take on two females at once."

"Pity." He grinned.

"I'm looking for a male. Hybrid. Was born with the name Tate. Came out of the Benson labs as an infant. His brother is called Ward, and he worked with Christopher. Maybe still does."

"The guy who turned on the Benson assholes and got Cammy and Ice out of that lab? We're looking for him. Sure he has a shitload of info to share about that assassin."

"Yeah, that's this Tate's younger brother." And Karen's son. Hopefully when they found him, he'd be willing to talk. Not to mention forgive the one who had given him life. Reaux slipped a piece of paper across the desk. "This has time, date, place of birth, possible coloring. Mother's name and situation."

Irek stared at it for a moment. "You want to know if he's dead or alive?"

Reaux nodded.

"And if he's alive…?"

"Just where to find him. Don't engage. Don't bring him here."

"You got it." He gave Reaux a broad smile. "So? When are we going out? New Orleans, or hell, even that shit bar in town? I could use a wingman."

Reaux sniffed. "You never needed a wingman."

"True. But I sure as shit enjoyed it."

"It's good to see you, brother."

"You too." He stood up, gave Reaux a hug.

"Hey, is there a back way out of here? It's a little crowded out there."

Irek knocked his chin in the direction of the open window. "Like old times."

Chuckling, Reaux headed straight for it. But just as he slipped through, he caught sight of a female and child walking hand in hand a few yards away. They were moving toward the bayou.

Karen and her cub.

CHAPTER 5

"Three, please," Karen told the grinning boy, his hands already caked with mud. "And make them extra thick."

"With cheese?" Caleb asked.

"Cheese, onions, pickles—"

"Ketchup and mustard?"

She laughed and spread the blanket on the damp ground, then opened the picnic basket. "Just make it the works, darling. Three mud cheeseburgers with everything on them. For here. Not to go."

He laughed too and took off down the shore. Before setting out the actual food she'd brought, Karen settled in on the thick rug and tucked her knees to her chest, inhaling the bayou deeply. A few hours ago the rain had cleared out, and left behind the most brilliant sunshine. She closed her eyes for a second and let it soak into her skin. It was warm for January. Had been for the past week. And she was going to enjoy it with her boy.

"He looks like you."

The male voice startled her, and she turned around. Reaux stood a few feet away. Where had he come from? And how hadn't she heard him? "Hey," she said.

He was dressed casually, in jeans, and a white T-shirt that molded to his broad chest and thick biceps. He looked relaxed. Handsome. Though seeing him shirtless and slightly sweaty the other day was pretty difficult to top.

Not that she should be thinking like that. Granted, she wasn't like the other females. She couldn't scent his musk. But she was a…female. And she had eyes. And a sex drive, even though she'd never gotten to use it. And Reaux was pretty much the sexiest male she'd ever encountered.

"I saw you heading this way and I thought…" He shrugged, and the corners of his mouth lifted into a grin.

"You'd check up on me?" Her heart flickered in her chest. Felt like a candle being lit. "That goes way beyond your duties as my 'ear.'"

His brows lifted. "Your ear."

"You know. I talk, you listen."

"Ah. Well this 'ear' was meeting up with a friend and I just saw you and the cub heading toward the bayou."

He sat down next to her, and once again that candle-flickering feeling erupted inside her. It was a strange and unfamiliar sensation. Not like what she was used to: fear or anxiety or dread.

"You hungry?" she asked him. "I have sandwiches and fruit. But Caleb is also whipping up some killer mudburgers."

"As tempting as that sounds…" His gaze moved

over her face. "I didn't come by to hijack your picnic lunch."

"No?"

He shook his head.

Something was happening. Between them. In the air. If she didn't know how strongly he felt about her not having sexual feelings for him, she would've sworn he wanted to kiss her. Granted, she hadn't been kissed all that much in her younger years, but a body knows.

"So...why did you come by?" she asked, and her tone was...playful. Flirtatious. She couldn't stop it. It was like she was silently inviting him to kiss her.

But before he could answer, before he could lean in and touch her lips with his, Caleb came running up. "Who are you?"

Reaux turned from her to address the boy. "Reaux."

"Are you a Pantera?"

"Breathe in through your nose, cub, and you tell me."

Caleb glanced at Karen and grinned, his eyes so heavy with excitement it made her belly clench. Then, under the blue afternoon bayou sky, her son closed his eyes and inhaled, trying to scent the puma within the male.

"Yes, you are!" he exclaimed.

Reaux smiled. "Very good. Your senses are strong."

Caleb beamed. "Can you shift?"

"Of course."

The boy's face fell. "I can't. Or I don't know how. I've tried. A few of the Hunters were teaching me, but it didn't work." He looked at Karen again and frowned. "Maybe I don't have a cat inside me."

He looked so devastated by this idea, Karen's stomach clenched. She knew he was interested and fascinated by the Pantera. And that he was curious about that part of himself. But until this moment, she hadn't realized just how deeply he wanted it.

"Caleb—" she began gently. But Reaux interrupted her.

"I didn't make my first shift until I was around your age. And I'm full Pantera." He gave the boy a stern look. "It will come to you. Soon. I can tell."

"Really?" Caleb exclaimed.

Karen looked at the male beside her. Was he being honest? Or just trying to assuage the boy's feelings.

"It's very important to be around pumas," Reaux continued, his focus remaining on Caleb. "They can help awaken your cat."

Caleb nodded, seeming to grow older in that very moment. "Okay. How about now?"

"Now?" the male repeated.

"Can I be around your puma?"

Reaux laughed. "I like this cub."

"Oh, Caleb," Karen began. "Reaux was just stopping by. He's not staying. Maybe another…"

Her words petered out because as she sat there, and as her enraptured son looked on, Reaux shifted into his cat. Where a second ago, a gorgeous dark-haired male with silver eyes sat beside her on the blanket, now there was a massive puma. Never in her life had she seen anything more beautiful. He was black as night, with streaks of white on his face. And when he turned to look at her, pierced her with silvery gray eyes, bared his teeth in what she was sure was an attempt to smile, her heart leapt into her throat.

My cat.

The thought was fleeting and crazy, and she refused to dissect it.

Reaux was moving away from her. Long, heavy strides and unsettlingly large paws. When he reached Caleb he rubbed his body against him. The boy fell down, and started laughing. The cat growled. Once. Then again.

Caleb looked over at her. "What should I do?"

"I think he wants to take you for a ride."

Scrambling to his feet, the boy looked like he'd just won the moon and stars. "Is it okay, mama?"

The puma glanced over its powerful shoulder and gave her a nod. But she didn't need it. Karen knew her boy was safe with Reaux, even in this form.

"Go," she told him. "I'll have the food ready when you get back."

Caleb squealed and climbed aboard.

As she watched the incredible beast race off down the shore with her heart on his broad back, Karen felt something rush from her body. She couldn't name it, but it was dark and bleak, and had grown happily inside her for years.

***

The puma liked the boy. It brought out the playful cub it once was. For an hour, they ran through the bayou. Following scent trails, digging in the earth.

The cat growled at the boy, trying to pull the young puma from him. It was there. Under the surface. It just needed to feel brave. But when the boy's mother called, a happy, playful sound bouncing off the cypress, the puma growled for the boy to climb on its back and away they went.
Back to the shore.
Back to his mother.

Reaux shifted the moment Caleb was off his back. Laid out before them was a small feast. Sandwiches, fruit, cookies. He watched as Karen settled her boy on the blanket and filled his plate. She asked about their adventures in the woods, and they laughed about the mudburgers being overdone and how they'd have to make do with the sandwiches this time around.

Cubs had been gone from the Wildlands for so long Reaux had forgotten what wonder they brought. Maybe someday he would be fortunate enough to have one. A family. A mate. It would be the greatest gift to watch someone mother her cub as she should. With maternal love, affection and joy and…blind acceptance.

How Karen mothered Caleb.

Besides being a breathtakingly beautiful woman, she was a deeply devoted mother. Even after what she'd been through. There was no anger or resentment placed on Caleb. She deserved happiness. She deserved a real, trustworthy mate who would hold her as she cried, as she released the pain caught inside her.

He snarled at the thought. No—at the vision of her 'good friend' Adrian taking on that role.

"What's wrong, Reaux?"

He glanced over at the picnic spread. Caleb was looking at him, curiously.

"I think he's hungry," Karen said. "Come sit down, Reaux. We have plenty."

Something was happening inside him. Something concerning. Yes, he'd agreed to help her, talk with her—try to show her ways to heal her grief and anger. But he wasn't stopping there. As he should. He was following her, playing with her son. Thinking about her as he lay in his bed at night. And right now... Right now there was nothing he wanted more than to change back into his cat, sniff out 'good friend' Adrian and fight the male until blood was shed.

"I wish I could," he told them. "But I have to go. I have a session." *Damn right, he did. With himself.*

Caleb looked disappointed, but Karen told him to return to his food and then she grabbed a sandwich and stood up. "Here. Take it with you."

She was too close. Her eyes eating him up. It was as though she were the one carrying the musk on her skin.

"My mama made it," Caleb called over to him. "Ham and cheese and mustard. She makes the best sandwiches ever."

Reaux's eyes caught hers. And held. "Ever?"

She blushed. Between that and her wild, windswept red hair, he was starting to forget his name. Who he was. Who she was to him.

"He's biased," Karen said, shaking her head. "Love colors our view, don't you think? And maybe seasons and sweetens as well."

"Maybe," he uttered.

Noting that he seemed preoccupied, she started to ask, "Reaux—"

But he cut her off. He needed to leave before he started to think he belonged here. With them. He feared his puma already felt that way. He glanced at Caleb. "Keep doing those exercises. Keep talking to him."

"Who?" Karen asked.

"My cat, mama," Caleb said.

"We can't be sure there's a cat inside you, honey," she reminded him. "We hope so, but—"

"Reaux's sure," the boy said, his expression resolute. "Right, Reaux?"

Reaux nodded. "You're Pantera, cub. I scent it."

"See," Caleb said. Then his face broke into a huge grin. "And what about mama, Reaux?"

"What about her?"

"What do you scent about her?"

Karen laughed, though her cheeks remained pink. "Don't be silly, Caleb. I have no puma inside me. There's nothing to smell—"

"Sweet mint," Reaux said.

They both turned to look at him. But it was only Karen's eyes he wanted in that moment.

"Everyone has a scent," he continued. "Your mama's is sweet mint."

"Is it the sweetest mint ever?" Caleb asked.

"Quite possibly."

"Maybe you should kiss her and find out."

"Caleb," Karen scolded, but her eyes never left Reaux's. "Sorry."

"Don't be," he said, his tone gruff and heavy with a need he hadn't felt in…Goddess, he didn't know how long. "I have to go."

She nodded. "Will I see you tomorrow?"

"That's why I came by," he lied.

"Oh. To make an appointment?"

He nodded, his flesh pulled tight against his muscle and bone. He was going to touch her, kiss her… He had to know how she tasted. "Ten o'clock?"

"I'll be there."

Without another word, every inch of him screaming with a fire she had set inside him, he broke from their sweet little gathering and gave himself over to his cat once again.

CHAPTER 6

Nightmares had been a normal part of life in the labs. One needed somewhere for the horrors of the day to go. But tonight, what was making Karen wake, cry out, breathe heavily—well, it had nothing to do with fear.

Shards of heat flickered in her belly as she opened her eyes. Dark room, moonlit ceiling. Her hand between her legs. Fingers wet. She could still see him—skull-shaved black hair, gray eyes, hard, passionate features and a mouth that had been where her fingers were now.

On a groan, she rolled to her side, her hand leaving her sex, and drew her knees up to her chest. Dreaming about him? God, she was getting in deeper and deeper with every passing day. She'd sworn to him that she didn't want him that way. And just that afternoon, she'd been silently begging him to kiss her.

What she needed to do was sleep, forget about this. Forget about what she wanted, what she could never have. And tomorrow, and the next day and the next, she'd work on herself. Being a better, stronger mother for her children.

It was near dawn when her wet and trembling body succumbed to exhaustion.

***

"Are you cold?" he asked her.

"Not at all. It's beautiful, actually." She smiled. "And I'm wearing my coat and drinking coffee. All good."

It was their fifth session, and Reaux had suggested they sit outside on the patio behind his office. For days, he'd been trying like hell to remain impassive and clinical with Karen, but it was proving impossible. The stories of what she'd been through were horrifying, yes, but they were also proof of what an incredible female she was. Brutally strong, fiercely protective.

Stunningly beautiful.

He'd never felt this way about anyone in his life, and it unnerved him. Letting a female in, allowing her access to his heart…it scared the shit out of him.

"Do you have many sessions out here?" she asked him, warming her hands on her coffee cup.

"A few."

"Caleb's been asking about you," she told him, a soft smile on her lips. "Wanting to go hunting for tracks again. He hasn't had fun like that in…ever. I can't tell you what it meant to me."

It had meant something to Reaux too. And that surprised him. The boy, the mother. The pair. "He's a fine cub." His voice sounded tired. He hadn't been sleeping well either.

"Did you mean it when you said you could scent a cat inside him?"

"Of course. I wouldn't say it if I didn't mean it. I'd never hurt him like that." When she looked relieved, even pleased, he remarked on it. "You want him to be able to shift, don't you?"

"He wants it," she clarified. "Desperately. And I want him to have one amazing thing come out of that hell."

She was amazing. Goddess, he was in trouble. "Are you prepared to be a mother to a puma shifter?"

"I am," she said with unwavering confidence. "Bring on the cat. And I plan on staying here. It's our home now, unless Raphael decides to kick us out or something..." She laughed, but stopped short when she saw his face. "What's wrong? You look...angry."

Reaux did a quick self eval. Anger? Yes. And at just the idea of Raphael sending this female away from the Wildlands. Away from him. Christ, it blazed inside him even now. Anger, possessiveness. What was happening to him?

And even as he asked the question, he knew the answer.

Karen was studying him with a slightly critical squint. "Are you like a few of your kind, Reaux?"

"What do you mean?"

"The anger...the questions about me being ready to be the mom of a shifter." Her pale brown eyes never left his for a minute. "Do you think we don't belong here? In the Wildlands? The rats, me, Caleb..."

He couldn't tell her what was going on in his head. In his heart. Hell, what he'd been feeling since the moment she'd nearly passed out by his door, then clung to him and cried her eyes out. This beautiful creature who made every inch of him go hard and hungry and possessive. This soulful mother, who knew how to love, and gave her boy everything she had. He couldn't tell her that he wanted her. That he was falling in love with her.

He placed her file on the tabletop and sighed. "I can't continue this. I'm sorry, Karen."

She looked down at the file, then back up at him. "What are you doing?"

"You need to find another Healer."

"No," she said sharply. "I want you."

Those words tore at his insides. He could image ten different scenarios where she was saying that to him. "I'm sorry. It's not working."

A sudden icy contempt flashed in her eyes. "Why not?"

Don't do it. Don't you fucking breathe a word. The woman before him had been through hell, and all she'd wanted from him was an ear and tools to help her heal. Instead he'd fallen in love with her. Last thing she needed was some alpha male panting after her, demanding to claim her and her boy. And if this—her and him—continued another day it was going to happen. Soft, sweet and gentle—that was reserved for patients. When he wanted something, he would go to any lengths to get it.

"What you're dealing with," he began, forcing a cool edge to his tone. "It requires a more experienced hand."

She blinked at him. "That's bullshit and you know it."

He ignored her. Had to. He stood up. "Like I said, I can recommend someone."

For long seconds she glared up at him as around them the sun warmed the cold bayou. Then she sniffed and shook her head. "I can't believe it, Reaux. You're a coward."

The word clawed at his gut. But again, he ignored her. "Good luck, Karen."

Brown eyes blazing, she stood too. "You still think I'm going to jump your bones, don't you?"

He didn't respond because at that very moment his asshole of a mind had grabbed onto that image and was going to town with it inside his head.

"You know," she said, her lovely face a mask of fury, "I've been nothing but professional. You're the one who came to my house and followed me down to the bayou and played with…" Teeth gritted, she shook her head. "Forget it. I just hadn't pegged you for a player."

And with that, she turned her coffee cup over and let the remaining brown liquid drench her patient file.

CHAPTER 7

Hunger gnawed at Karen's belly as she headed over to her favorite cypress with her lunch in hand. She hadn't eaten breakfast. Too late getting up in the morning. Again. It was all those sleepless nights.

She blamed them on him.

She tucked into the cypress and opened her bag, took out a sandwich. It had been a week since she'd walked out on Reaux, and she'd been trying to avoid seeing him ever since. Which wasn't easy as they worked in the same building. But she'd managed it. Boy, had she been a fool. Believing that Reaux was her safe place. That maybe he cared about her. And the whole time he was just thinking she was like every other female: unable to control her urges around him.

Well, she could control her urges!

Hell, she'd controlled them for twelve long years.

She ate part of her sandwich, but barely tasted it. She put it down on the napkin and picked up her fruit. Sucked. This whole thing. How long did it take to get over a…crush? The answer never made it to her brain because just as she was tossing a slice of apple into her mouth, her sandwich was stolen. Right in front of her. By a black puma with threads of white on its face.

Karen stared at it. At him. Her heart in her throat. "What's all this?" she said in a hard tone. "Trying to scare me off Wildlands property?"

The puma gulped down the sandwich in one bite, then started pacing in front of her.

"I'm not going anywhere, Reaux," she said, packing up the rest of her lunch. "This is my home."

He snarled at her, but kept pacing.

"What did I ever do to you? Seriously?" Her eyes formed tears. God, she was a wimp now. What happened to that hard woman with the layers of metal around her?

As she stood up, the cat froze, then gloriously shifted. Back into the male she was so desperate to forget. Six feet of gorgeous, fearsome alpha male stood there, his steely gray eyes impaling her.

"I'm sorry I sought you out, okay?" she told him through her stupid, pointless tears. "I'm sorry I forced you to see me, help me."

He stalked toward her, took her shoulders in his large hands.

"But it wasn't—" Her voice cracked. "Isn't because I want to jump you."

"I believe you."

Her eyes lifted to meet his. So dark and compelling. "What? But I thought…"

"It was never your desire that worried me, Karen. It was mine."

Her lips parted, but she didn't say anything.

"I wanted you from the moment I met you. Something new for me. And honestly, it scared the shit out of me." He shook his head, nostrils flaring. "I couldn't stop thinking about you. Still can't."

Her chest felt so tight. With wonder and anxiety, and…hope. "Then why…all that coldness and pushing me away?"

He brought his hand up and cupped her face, brushed his thumb over her cheek. "You needed time to heal, space…release from your anger and grief. All I could think about was having you. I was no good for you as a Healer."

"That's so not true," she said, pressing her cheek into his hand. "And for the record, I get to make those decisions for myself. I know what I need."

His eyes searched hers, trying to read her thoughts. "What's that?"

"You," she said simply.

A gleam of mischievous heat crossed his gaze. "I thought you said you didn't want to jump my bones?"

She shrugged playfully. "Yes, but I didn't say anything about you jumping mine."

He tipped her face up. "Karen…"

"They've never been jumped before."

He closed his eyes for a second and inhaled. "You're killing me."

"I've never felt like this about anyone, Reaux."

His lids lifted and he was right there again. Such intensity, such promise. Such a male.

She smiled. "I swear I'm still seventeen in some ways. I don't know how to react. What to say when I really like a boy."

"That's it right there," he said, lowering his mouth to hers, and taking her in a soft, sweet kiss.

Karen melted against him, feeling both his hard muscle and the soft heat of his lips. She'd only been kissed once or twice before she was taken. But she hardly remembered it. How it had felt. Surely it was nothing compared to this.

Reaux released her face and his arms stole around her. He pulled her close and, as the bayou breeze blew cold and fresh around them, he kissed her so thoroughly, so hungrily, she forget for a moment where she was. Who she was.

When he eased back, they were just a breath away. Blurry. Their breath co-mingling.

"You do that really well," she whispered.

He grinned. "So do you."

"Thank you. It's only my second or third time."

"Oh, Karen...*ma chère*..." He dropped his head and kissed her bottom lip, sending a rush of heat through her belly. "This is dangerous."

"Why? We're just kissing."

A soft growl hummed in his throat. "It's different for Pantera than it is for humans. It means more. Especially to the male." He leaned in close to her ear and lapped at the lobe with his tongue. She shivered. "Come..." he uttered. And when she gasped, he chuckled. "Out with me tonight."

"Oh." She laughed softly. "Like a date?"

"Yes." He took her lobe into his mouth and sucked it gently. "Damn, woman, you taste good."

Heat coiled in Karen's sex and her nipples hardened against her bra. If Reaux had wanted to take things further, she wasn't sure she'd have the strength to remember they were out in public, during the day.

"I've never been on a date before," she said breathlessly as he continued to nip at her ear.

That revelation had him pulling back suddenly. His eyes caught hers and held. They were dark and deep, but soft as a caress. "Does it make me a bastard if I want to claim all of your firsts?"

She shook her head. It was truly all she could manage in that moment. She felt strange and wonderful, and like she was made of air. Like she could float away.

"I'll pick you up at six," he said, releasing her, a grin the size and intensity of the sun on his handsome face.

Would she truly float away? No. No. She had to stay here. On Earth. In the Wildlands. For him. And their date.

Awareness and urgency coursing through her blood, she watched him walk away, watched him shift. Watched his glorious beast thunder across the mossy landscape. As her mind conjured only one word to describe him.

Mine.

***

"Why do you keep doing this to yourself?" Irek chided as Reaux stalked through the door of the spy's office inside the garden house, a trio of female growls echoing behind him. "I know you want the info, but I also know how crazy the sexual fanfare makes you."

It did make him crazy, Reaux thought, dropping into the chair opposite his friend's desk. Or it normally did. Today, though, it was odd—he hardly noticed the stares, the sounds of blatant desire as he passed.

Maybe it was because his mind was focused on the need of only one female. The one he wanted.

The one he intended to make his mate.

"You said you had something for me?" Reaux said distractedly.

"I do." Irek was never one to sugarcoat, and his dark mask of regret was troubling. "Some tough news, my friend."

Dread slithered up Reaux's spine, and all he could see in his mind was Karen's face. "What?"

"This was a hard dig," Irek told him. "Had to call in a few favors with some ex-Benson employees. Two who used to work there around the time the cub was born. Seems he was adopted by a couple related to Christopher."

So much for not sugarcoating. This had to be bad. "He's dead, isn't he?"

"Didn't make it past day ten."

"Fuck…"

"Cub needed his mother. Pantera cubs, they have to have that bond. Some more than others. Sorry, my brother."

For a second, Reaux just sat there, trying like hell to think of a way to break the news to Karen. He hadn't even told her he was looking into it. But she deserved to know the truth, as terrible as it was. So, what did he do? Head over there right now? Wait for tonight? For their date?

He stood up. There was no good time. "I appreciate it, brother."

"Anytime. You know that." Irek got up too and embraced him, gave him a couple of hard knocks to the back before releasing him. "You going out the window today?"

Reaux shook his head. "No. I'm good." He left the way he came in, this time so preoccupied with his woman and the news he'd just heard that he didn't even hear the hungry calls of the females who bracketed him.

CHAPTER 8

"My hair looks insane," Karen complained as she stared into the full-length mirror on the inside of her closet door.

"No it doesn't," Indy insisted from her self-proclaimed 'safe' place on the edge of the bed. She'd come over for moral support, and boy was she giving it all she had.

Unfortunately, Karen was way too nervous and excited to believe her friend's positive feedback.

"And what color is this lipstick?" Pointing to her lips, she rounded on Indy. "Slutastic?"

Indy sprang from the bed. "Okay, you're freaking out. And you need to not."

"Easy for you to say. You have Angel. It's done. You're happy." She stared at the woman, brows creeping together. "Right? You're happy?"

"Blissful." Her eyes took on an instant dreamy look. "Can't believe it's possible, but wow. Bliss. Full."

Karen pushed out her bottom lip in a mock pout. "I want that."

Quickly coming out of her love coma, Indy reached out and put her hands on her friend's shoulders. "You're about to have that. He's on his way over here."

Little tendrils of excitement exploded inside Karen. Again. "We're just going out on a date. One date."

"Uh huh."

Karen laughed, and for a second, it eased some of the pressure that had been building inside her since…well, since she'd met Reaux.

"You don't know these Pantera males like I do, hon," Indy said, grabbing Karen's sweater off the back of the chair. "They're not casual daters. They see something they like, that they want, they go after it. It's a puma thing. See a nice, juicy, female in sight? They're claiming it."

Karen snorted at her. "Way to paint a picture. Nice and juicy, huh?"

Indy grinned wickedly. "Oh, yeah, if he knows what he's doing, that is. And Pantera males, going by my own, they know."

Laughing, Karen rolled her eyes at the sexual innuendo, but inside her humming body, every muscle was clenching. She was so ready. So willing. "Okay." She held her arms out, did a quick turnaround. "How do I look? And don't lie because you feel sorry for me and what I went through in the lab."

"Well if I can't lie…" Indy began, her eyes twinkling with humor. She did a slow visual sweep. From straight, shiny hair to black strapless dress to peekaboo heels. "You look gorgeous."

Karen let out a tiny squeal. "Swear?"

"Double swear."

Then she sobered. "Let's hope he thinks so."

"Honey," Indy started, helping Karen with her sweater. "Did you not hear what I said about Pantera males? He's into you. He wouldn't be—"

There was a decided rap on the front door.

Indy laughed. "On your porch right now if he didn't want to eat you alive." She winked. "You know what I mean."

"Oh god." Karen absolutely knew. In fact, as she hurried to the door, her skin was literally trembling with awareness. Yes, yes, yes, she was ready for that: dinner, conversation, and later, being eaten alive.

Her smile broke wide and excited as she pulled back the thick wood. But it faltered slightly as she saw Reaux standing there. He looked breathtakingly handsome. He was wearing black jeans, black boots, a dark green button-down shirt, and lord have mercy, he was holding a single lavender lily in his hands.

"Evening, beautiful," he said, handing her the flower.

"Thank you," she said, slightly breathless. "It's so pretty."

His gaze raked over her hungrily. "Nothing compared to you." He whistled softly and shook his head. "Wow."

Karen smiled. As she'd told him earlier, she'd never been on a date before. She also hadn't been wooed. Admired. Flirted with. And the feeling was overwhelming. In the best way possible. She felt…young again. Not that she was some crone at thirty, or anything, but the years in that cell had passed painfully slowly. They felt longer than they were. And now, as she stood here under the wolfish—no, the cat-ish—gaze of her Pantera male, she had a new and thrilling lease on life. And fun. And…hopefully sex.

"You both ready?" Reaux asked her.

"Both?" Karen repeated, suddenly confused.

He glanced past her. "Isn't Caleb coming?"

Her heart leapt into her throat. Had he really come there hoping to take them both…? "I thought it was just us. Caleb's going to hang out with Adrian tonight. You remember my friend, Adrian?"

Reaux nodded, a shadow crossing his steely gray gaze. Then he seemed to recall something, and he took a thin envelope out of his pocket and handed it to her. "I brought this for him."

"A CD?" she said.

"Don't laugh…"

"I wouldn't dare. Unless, you know, it's supposed to be funny."

"I'm a big music lover. Have been since I was a kid." He leaned his powerful body against the door and lowered his voice. "These are the songs I listened to back in the day."

"What day is that?" she asked, knowing she was flirting. With her voice, her eyes.

He inhaled deeply. "When I was trying to…" He looked away for a second. "Get my cat to come out."

The light flirtation she had been enjoying up until that moment gave way to something else entirely. Something deeper, and hopefully longer-lasting. It was the realization of what this male had not only given to her son, but created for him. And it spread over and through her like the softest, warmest, safest blanket.

"I'll make sure he gets it," she promised, her voice thankful and resolute.

He nodded. "Hungry?" he asked, one dark brow raised.

You have no idea, male. "Very."

He smiled and offered her his arm. "Let's go."

***

"You didn't," Karen said, laughing in between sips of her wine.

"I was a little devil," Reaux told her as he watched her across the table. "The teacher made me eat every last bite."

"Did you get sick afterwards?"

"In ways I refuse to talk about because I plan on kissing you later and I don't want that image of me stuck in your mind."

She laughed again. "Fair enough."

Not wanting to take Karen out of the Wildlands, Reaux had decided to bring her to Miss Nathalie's. A few months ago, the older female had decided to turn her boarding house into a restaurant. There were so many new couples now, new faces in the Wildlands, the female had caved to the demand for a nice eating spot. Not that the eight-table spot was all that fancy, but it did have some seriously good food and a killer romantic atmosphere.

"What about you?" Reaux asked, taking in the way the candle flickering between them on the table made her eyes glow amber. "What bad stuff did you do as a kid?"

The question sobered her for a moment, and Reaux wondered if maybe he'd overstepped. But she quickly relaxed and said, "I used to record my parents sleeping."

Reaux put down his beer. "I'm sorry, what was that again?"

She laughed. "Both of them claimed they didn't snore. I got so sick of hearing that argument." She shrugged, her pretty pale shoulders lifting and lowering. "I recorded them. Then I played it for the whole neighborhood."

"I bet you got in trouble."

"You'd think, right?" She picked up her fork. "But my parents weren't like that. They were both really caring and loving—and forgiving." She stabbed a tiny carrot and slipped it into her mouth. "And they could take a joke."

Lucky, lucky, carrot. "They sound like good people."

"They were." When tears suddenly sprang to her eyes, he reached across the table and took her hand. "I swear, I don't know what's wrong with me," she said, shaking her head. "I didn't cry more than a handful of times during the twelve years I was in the lab. And now I'm out and free and...happy." She smiled at that. "And a walking tear duct."

"It's a good thing, Karen," he assured her. "Means you're healing. You're allowing yourself to heal."

Her eyes lifted to meet his, and they were thoughtful as well as glistening. "What do you want, Reaux?" When one of his eyebrows lifted, she smiled softly. "I mean, out of life?"

Well, that was a question. Especially now. Meeting her had changed everything for him. "I want the Pantera and the Wildlands to be safe."

She nodded. "Agreed."

He squeezed her hand. "And I'd like a mate and a family."

She swallowed. He watched the movement in her throat. "You deserve that," she told him with absolute sincerity. "After how your mother treated you. Have you..." She cleared her throat. "Have you ever come close to finding a mate?"

"No." His eyes were locked on hers.

"Oh."

His lips twitched with gentle amusement. "Not until recently anyway."

"Oh." She smiled.

Goddess, he wanted to kiss her. Could he get away with it here? He grinned to himself. Not with the kind of kissing he had in mind. Not just a peck across the table.

Two females came into the dining room then. Up until that point, it had been all couples, which hadn't presented a problem for Reaux. But this, he sighed...this could be a problem.

It didn't take long for them to catch sight of him or to ask to be seated close by.

"I'm done if you are," Karen said.

Reaux's gaze slid back to her. She understood completely.

"But you haven't had dessert yet," he said, bringing her hand to his mouth and kissing it.

She shrugged. "I have ice cream in my freezer."

"Really?"

She nodded, smiling and biting her lip.

He looked at her with hooded eyes. "I love ice cream."

"Then let's get out of here, male."

Her words caused the puma inside him to snarl and scratch. It wanted out and at her. Cage yourself, he told it. *We don't want to scare her.*

He stood, and went to pull back her chair. And after paying the check, he led the woman who was to become his mate through the dining room and out the door, utterly and completely oblivious to the two females staring after him.

CHAPTER 9

Karen stood in Adrian's living room, Reaux beside her, trying to pretend there wasn't a *vibe* happening between the two males. But it wasn't easy. Reaux was acting all possessive of her, while Adrian was being territorial. And all the while, Caleb continued to sleep on the couch.

"Listen, I haven't found anything," Adrian said, his focus totally on Karen. "But you know I'll keep looking."

"Thank you," she said, nodding. "And thanks for taking care of Caleb tonight."

"Anytime." He punched the word to make sure she really got it. "You want me to carry him home?"

"I've got him," Reaux said, already heading that way, scooping up the sleeping boy and cradling him in his arms.

Adrian sniffed. "I was only suggesting it because he knows me."

"He knows me, too," Reaux returned with a thread of barely disguised aggression. "And even more importantly, his cat knows me."

This took Adrian by surprise, and he turned to look at Karen. "He's…shit, Kar, he shifted?"

She gave him a quick smile. "No. Not yet.

"He's Pantera," Reaux said, already striding toward the front door. "And if they're in tune, one Pantera can scent another. He'll learn all about what he is."

"I'm guessing you're going to teach him," Adrian countered icily.

Reaux held the door open for Karen. "Already there, brother."

"I think we should go," Karen said quickly. Forget strained. It was like a testosterone explosion going on in here. She knew Adrian was protective of her, but this was ridiculous. And she wasn't at all sure what Reaux was doing besides acting like an impolite jerk. "Thanks again," she told her friend as they headed out the door.

"Like I said, Kar," he called after her. "Anytime."

As they moved away from the house, down the walkway and onto the path toward her place, Karen could feel the heat off the male beside her. Not a gentle, soothing heat. But a fire that needed to be extinguished.

"Okay, what the hell is wrong with you, Reaux?" She glanced over at him. His jaw was tight.

"That male's in love with you," he ground out.

"No. He's not."

He sniffed darkly. "I'm a professional, Karen."

"A professional what?"

"This isn't funny."

"Oh come on. It's a little funny." Two massive gold cats came running past them. Reaux didn't even acknowledge their presence. "Listen, Love Doctor, Adrian is dating a Hunter."

That didn't deter him one little bit. "You can date people, sleep with people…"

"Point?"

"Doesn't mean they're the one."

"You're very philosophical for a shrink."

He stopped on the trail, a block from her little house, and turned to face her. Caleb was still sound asleep in his arms. His eyes blazed down at her. "You're not taking this seriously."

"No, I'm not. Because I'm not in love with him and that's all that matters."

Reaux stared at her, nostrils flaring.

"And furthermore—" she continued hotly.

"I get a furthermore?"

"Furthermore," she pressed. "I'm already interested in someone."

The blaze in his eyes upgraded to inferno. "Really?"

She nodded. Slowly. Then broke out the easy, flirtatious smile. "It's a terrible crush, actually."

It took him a moment to get there, for his eyes to gentle and his lips to twitch. "I'm sorry."

"Yep. I don't see myself getting over it." Her gaze moved over his face. "Unless, of course, that guy doesn't feel the same about me."

Reaux exhaled heavily, shook his head. And then before either of them could say another word, he leaned in—boy in his arms—and kissed her. Nothing hungry, nothing possessive, but slow and drugging and filled with promises.

"He feels the same," he whispered against her lips. "That guy." He smiled. "He feels unquestionably, unabashedly, unreservedly the same."

And then he kissed her for a full five minutes in the middle of the path before they finally broke apart and headed for home.

***

Reaux slid the covers up to the cub's chin, then paused a moment. Is this what it felt like? To be a parent? A father? Caleb looked totally at peace, cheek pressed against his pillow, so trusting. *He has a mother who would die for him.* Reaux smiled. *Lucky boy. To have such a female love you.*

The scent of mint tickled Reaux's nostrils and he instantly growled softly.

"Is he all right?" Karen whispered, coming up beside him.

He was more than all right. "I can sense it in him. His cat. It's very strong-willed."

She laughed softly. "I'm not surprised."

Her quick sigh brought his head around. "What is it?"

"I wish I could sense it. I feel like I have nothing to offer him in that way. No understanding."

Reaux slipped his arm around her waist and eased her to him. "You have more important gifts to give him. Love. Security. Acceptance. You have no idea what those things mean to a young male."

Her eyes searched his. "Or to an older male?"

"Yes," he breathed. Goddess, his heart was full. He needed to tell her. How he felt. What he wanted.

But what if she didn't want him? Just the idea had his insides aching. A strange and terrifying feeling. He'd never realized until now how he'd rejected mating. Used his 'curse' as an excuse never to get close.

When Caleb rolled to his side and coughed, Karen made a let's-get-out-of-here gesture with her head, and they left the room.

"Ice cream?" she whispered, closing the boy's door and heading into the hallway.

"Definitely." He followed her into the small kitchen, then leaned on the counter and watched as she scooped green chocolate mint into two bowls. Afterwards, they stole back into the living room and dropped down on the sofa.

"I like your house," he said, glancing around. "Comfortable."

"It's one of the new cottages for us rats and hybrids. Not that it's huge or anything," she continued in between bites of ice cream. "But to me it feels massive. After living in that cage for so long."

His cat dragged its claws down Reaux's spine. It wanted out, wanted to kill every single being that had hurt this female. "You're free now," he said. "In so many ways."

"I'm just starting to feel that." Sudden happiness bubbled in her eyes and she said, completely without restraint, "Do you want to stay over?"

Reaux's skin went tight, and his appetite for ice cream evaporated. "Are you sure?"

She nodded. "I am. I've never slept with anyone before. In the same bed."

"Neither have I," he told her.

She smiled broadly, almost conspiratorially. "So, you want to?"

The puma jumped, but Reaux pushed it back. What it wanted to say was, *I don't want to ever leave your side. You're mine.* But that would sound dire and desperate, and frankly, he'd been an overbearing asshole of an alpha while they'd walked home, over the Adrian issue.

But then again, he was Pantera. A male. A predator at his core. And he'd found the one he wished to mate. How could he not show her that?

"Well?" she pressed, her eyes bright with excitement.

"I'd love to stay," he said. And when she smiled again, he smiled back.

After they finished their ice cream and put the bowls in the sink, Karen showed Reaux the bathroom, gave him a spare toothbrush, then went into her room to change.

Reaux had brought nothing, so when he came out, he was wearing only his boxers. "Didn't bring my overnight bag."

Dressed in a thick, pink robe, Karen stood by the window. Her eyes moved over him covetously. "You're fine. Really…fine." She chewed her lip. "If you're comfortable, I'm comfortable. You look…"

"Fine?" he asked.

She let out a groan. "I don't know why I'm so nervous."

"First sleepover. For both of us." He got under the covers and reached for her. "Come here."

Before his greedy eyes, she slipped off her robe and came over to the bed. Reaux practically swallowed his tongue at the sight. The woman was a goddess.

Forget lingerie. She had on a sort of long pink tank that hit mid-thigh. Showed off her toned arms, perfect breasts, tight nipples, small waist and long legs. She was sexy as hell, but cute too.

Christ, was he drooling?

The instant she slipped under the covers, the instant her warm body moved against his, he eased her close. *Mine.* And when she draped her leg across his thigh and pressed her cheek to his chest, Reaux, for the first time in his life, knew true contentment.

"Thanks for our date," she whispered, her breath tickling the skin on his chest.

His fingers played in her hair. So soft. "Anytime."

"And carrying the kid home, putting him to bed."

"Of course."

"And…well, putting me to bed, too." She tipped her face up, then, to see him. "Reaux?"

He tucked a strand of hair behind her ear. "Mmmm hmmm?"

"I want to rip your clothes off now."

He laughed. Couldn't help himself. "I'm not wearing much, *ma chère*. And if we were anywhere else, I'd let you. Goddess, I ache for you. You have no idea. I can't wait to taste you." He growled softly and kissed her hungrily, deeply, then whispered as he pulled back, "These lips as well as the others."

She groaned and pressed her core against his thigh.

A snarl ripped from his lips. "My cat wants you as badly as I do. But I think we should just sleep tonight. Caleb is so close by, and Pantera males aren't quiet."

She groaned, her eyes heavy with desire as she stared at him. But in the end, she nodded.

"Rest now." He gathered her in his arms. "We have plenty of time."

We have a lifetime, my beautiful mate, he thought as she tucked into his shoulder and released a weighty breath.

CHAPTER 10

Sunlight warmed her face, while the heat and muscles of a delicious male scorched her back. Karen grinned. Reaux was tucked in behind her, and there was nothing she wanted more in that moment than for him to slip his arm around her waist and yank her back even closer. So she could feel every bit of him. Warm breath near her neck. Hard cock against the rise of her buttocks.

She could get used to this.

If she moved, arched her back just so, maybe she could entice him to…

She heard Caleb. He was in the living room. Talking and playing with his little army men. No arched back this morning.

We have plenty of time.

Reaux's words, his promise, hummed through her. Never had she wanted anything more. She couldn't wait to have him, and be taken by him. She couldn't wait to connect with him. She was falling in love with him.

The sound of something hitting the ground in the living room had her gently disentangling herself from his grasp. Trying not to wake him, she slipped out of bed and grabbed her robe. She found Caleb sprawled out on the living room rug, a big book on the ground beside him. He looked up the second she came in.

"Is Reaux here, mama?"

She felt strange answering that question. Was it okay? That Reaux was here, in her house, in her bed? Waking up with her? In her mind and heart, she believed Reaux to be her mate. It's what she wanted. What she believed he wanted too. A soft smile touched her mouth. "Yes, baby."

"Oh, good," the boy said, his eyes lighting up like two firecrackers. "I want to tell him I played the CD two times last night."

"That's wonderful, honey," she said, coming over and ruffling his hair.

"And did you feel your puma, cub?" came a deep male voice behind them.

Karen turned and promptly swooned. Standing there, his big body taking up residence in her small living room, was the sexiest male in the whole wide world. He was wearing his jeans again, but no shirt, and his shoulders, chest and belly were tantalizingly ripped with hard muscle. She checked her mouth for possible drool, then grinned. Was he truly hers? Could he be hers? As she gazed into his eyes, so predatory and passionate as he strode toward her, she felt he wanted to be.

"My puma needs to hear it again, Reaux!" Caleb called out.

"Then break out the music, cub," he said with a happy growl, coming up behind Karen and giving her a quick kiss on the neck. "Denying your beast can be a very dangerous thing."

Blazing heat and tickling shivers moved through Karen's already sensitive body. When he was good and truly hers, he could spend every night there, in her bed. Their bed. She'd have to get a bigger bed. Fit for a long, heavily muscled Pantera.

"What's for breakfast, mama?" Caleb asked.

She looked down at him, lovingly. "You're hungry?"

"Yep. And so's my cat." He growled at her for effect.

She glanced over her shoulder at Reaux, who was staring at her neck. "What about you, male? Hungry?"

His eyes lifted to capture hers. "Starving."

Her pulse jumped and skittered in her blood. "You two hang out, then, and I'll whip up something."

"Need help?" he asked with an intimate smile.

"Maybe later," she said, returning it.

"Definitely later."

Though her body was a jumble of awareness, happiness, tension and wonder, Karen managed to gathered up her ingredients. As she cracked eggs and toasted bread, she took in the sweet little wonderful world she was living in at that moment. Male and cub, playing on the rug, laughing as their army men strategized and battled. Was this a home? The real kind? With a…family in it? Or could it be? Her heart pinged with its familiar sense of loss. All that was missing was Ward and Tate. Reaux could teach them so much. As if she'd called out to him, he glanced up then and caught her looking at him. His eyes were steady and sure, his grin hungry and predatory. Her heart skipped, then melted. This male was her heart, her home. She prayed he felt it too.

With a contented sigh, she went back to frying her bacon, and the boys went outside. Everything was going to work out, she mused as she watched them run, watched Reaux shifting in and out of his cat every few minutes. It had to work out. After what she'd been through over the past twelve years, she deserved something real and wonderful.

She deserved Reaux.

She deserved a happy and whole family.

She quickly set the table, plated all the food, and was about to grab milk and juice when Reaux's cellphone, which he'd left on the counter the night before, buzzed. She grabbed it, and was about to run out and give it to him when she caught sight of the readout. A dark sickness crept over her, and all at once the pleasure and safety from a moment ago evaporated.

The info I gave u was flawed. K's cub was 15 days old when he died. Not 10. Sry for the f-up.

Karen stared at it, eyes so wide, brow so furrowed, it soon became painful. K was her. The cub who died had to be Tate. Suddenly breathless, she had this strange urge to get into the corner, huddle down and stay there. For hours. Days. Weeks? But she didn't. Couldn't. Caleb wasn't going to see her like that ever again.

She glanced up. Looked outside. At her son and

Reaux. Running around the yard. She'd trusted this male. With everything she had. Her child, her heart. Why would she do that? After everything she'd been through...why would she do that?

Caleb burst through the door then, his cheeks pink from the cold morning air. "We're starving, mama!"

She nodded, forced a smile. "I'll bring it out to you. Can you ask Reaux to come in and help me?"

"Yep!"

A few seconds later, the male she'd believed was her true mate only minutes ago strode in, a wide grin on his face. "He's so close. I can't wait to see his first shift."

"You left your phone on the counter."

He immediately tensed. Not because of the phone, but because of the tone in her voice. Eyeing her closely, he took it from her hand. And when he read the text, he cursed and shook his head.

"You need to go," she said.

"Karen—"

"Go. Now."

"I was going to tell you."

"Before or after you slept with me?"

"That's not fair."

"Your shirt's in the bathroom," she said. "Shoes too."

"Don't do this. Don't go there in your head."

She glared at him, hissed at him. "Don't tell me what to do. Ever. How long have you been keeping this from me?"

He reached for her. "I haven't been keeping anything from you."

"Don't touch me." Tears broke in her eyes. "My Tate? He's...dead. All this time."

Reaux reached for her again. "Please let me hold you."

She shook her head, tears streaming down her face. "You need to go. Caleb has been through hell. He doesn't deserve to walk in on this."

"Karen..." For several seconds, it looked like Reaux might fight her. His eyes held a deep misery, deep regret. But after a moment, he went into the bathroom and grabbed his shirt. When he came out, he went straight for her. "I asked a friend for help. That's all. I wanted to give you this. I wanted to do this for you. I'm in love with you, Karen." He dragged a hand through his hair. "I found out this information late yesterday. I was going to tell you. But last night...I don't know. I guess I just wanted us both to be happy." He stared at her, waiting for a response. When she didn't give one, he cursed again and headed for the door. "It's easy to jump back into dark feelings and even darker assumptions. Believe me, I know."

Tears streaked down her cheeks as he walked out the door. But she quickly wiped them away. Her son needed her. Whole and happy. And if she had to, hiding her pain once again. It was a state of being she knew all too well.

***

It had been two days.

Two long, suckass days since Reaux had seen her. And he'd never felt more miserable in his life.

"We need you to profile him, Reaux."

Reaux glanced up. The leader of the Pantera, along with Parish and three Suits—Genevieve, Roch and Irek—were in his office. Morning meeting.

"By some miracle from the Goddess," Raphael continued, "Xavier managed to locate and save the research from the computers that were blown up by the suicide bomber. He explained it all to me, but frankly the Geeks speak a different language."

"Those plans are disturbing as fuck," Parish ground out. The leader of the Hunters was pacing near the window. "Just like the madman who created them.

"If Christopher realizes we managed to salvage the data," Irek put in, "he could unleash the virus on the Wildlands. We need to get to him."

Reaux released a weighty breath. His head needed to be in this game. The lives of his kind were at stake. "You want to know everything about a man who would do this?" When they all nodded, he added, "I'll create a profile, but you have to know it'll be an educated guess."

"We know," Genevieve told him. "Work with Mackenzie and Lux on this." She handed him a zip drive. "Here's everything we have on him so far, but we'd ultimately like your opinions on where he might be living now, how he spends his money, who he spends his time with. Anything and everything."

"To what end exactly?" Reaux asked her.

"To locate the fucker." Parish leaned back against the wall and crossed his arms over his chest. "We're taking him out for good. And everyone who works for him."

Understanding dawning quickly, a low growl rumbled from Reaux's chest. "That's why you've called the Pantera home?" He eyed Raphael. "You're assembling an army."

The leader of the Pantera didn't deny it. "We're done with pairs going in, putting on Band-Aids and putting out fires. We're going to end this."

"Good." Before Reaux could respond further, there was a knock on the door. Then it opened slightly and Karen's face appeared. When she realized who was inside, she grimaced. "Sorry. I'll come back later."

Reaux was out of his seat in seconds. "No. We're done."

Raphael gave his cousin a look. "We need it by tonight."

"You'll have it," he assured him as the group got up and filed out of his office.

When he and Karen were finally alone, he rounded on her. "Hey. You okay?"

She looked pensive, pale, as she sat down in one of the leather chairs. "I wonder if you could help me."

His brow drifted up. "Of course. Anything."

"I need a Healer." Her eyes lifted to meet his. "And you're the best there is."

CHAPTER 11

The look on Reaux's face cut her deep. Confused, eager, strained. She knew she'd hurt him. From the moment he'd walked out of her house two days ago, she'd known. Just as she'd known that what he'd done for her, finding out the truth about Tate, had been done because he cared about her.

Maybe even loved her.

Heart squeezing with hope, she gazed up at him. He was standing, his back to his desk, arms crossed over his broad chest. He looked gorgeous and pensive.

"I'm so sorry," she began. "You were right. I'm skittish, afraid of being in pain again. Afraid of getting hurt. Afraid of trusting. Afraid of grieving." She inhaled sharply, her eyes begging him to see what was in her heart. "But I will, and I am."

For several long seconds, Reaux stared at her, his eyes darkening with emotion. Then he shook his head. "I should've told you. Right away. Soon as I found out."

"Hey, I get why you didn't." She gave him a soft smile. "We were having a night. First one like that for the both of us in a long time. It was beautiful and perfect and fun. You wanted to be happy. You wanted to see me happy."

He pushed away from the desk, came over to her, knelt down in front of her. "I'm so sorry about Tate."

Tears pricked her eyes. Those damn tears. But at least they were coming now. Healing her as Reaux had said. Helping her see the truth. See the love and happiness and future she could have if she embraced it. "Thank you," she said, reaching for his hand. "For looking. For getting answers for me." She threaded her fingers with his. "They may not have been the ones I wanted. But at least I know."

Reaux's eyes blazed into hers with heat and intensity. "I love you, woman. You and the cub. I want you as my family."

She couldn't speak. Tears only.

"Please don't kick me out of your life again," he uttered. "My puma's fiercely tender heart can't take it."

Never, she mused. *You're mine.*
And I'm yours.

It was time to show him.

She released his hand. Silently, she stood up and went to the door. With a quick flick of the wrist, she locked it, then turned back to face him. Slowly, sensuously, she started to take off her clothes. She hadn't planned this, but it was right. So right.

Reaux had come to his feet and was watching her with hooded eyes. With every piece of clothing she removed and tossed over the chair, those eyes darkened. "Here?" he asked, his tone husky and thick with need.

"Can you think of a better place?" she asked, grinning as she slipped out of her bra and panties and stood before him naked.

The snarl that answered her was terrifying. And sexy. And so Reaux she shivered.

He came at her like a predator—the predator he was—scooping her up in his arms and taking her mouth under his. He kissed her hard and hungry, and like he hadn't seen her in a year. And Karen melted into him, giving herself over to his intensity. He tasted like heaven, sweet and mysterious, and when his fingers pressed into her skin and his tongue invaded her mouth, a gasp broke from her throat.

"That's right, Karen," he snarled against her lips. "You're mine. Say it. Tell me."

"All yours, Reaux," she uttered, her skin on fire, her sex clenching and wet.

He kissed her again, a punishing kiss that had her crying out softly, had her gripping his shoulders. She wanted his clothes off too. Needed to feel his skin, against her hands, under her nails. On top of her as he thrust deeply inside of her.

"Goddess, I've thought about this," he uttered, biting at her lower lip, then suckling it deep. "You, naked in my arms. The scent of your pussy in my nostrils."

His words, so graphic and honest, sent her body into a panic. Heat coursed through her, and she tried to yank at his clothes. *Off. Off. Off.*

Get inside. Get inside where it's warm. Where you belong.

Feeling her urgency, he chuckled darkly,

hungrily, then set her down on the rug. Above her, the skylight blasted her with warm sunlight. Around her, the green freshness of the bayou lulled her. In front of her, standing at her feet, naked… Cut and chiseled and so long and hard, her mouth watered. God! Goddess! Whoever had created this creature…Reaux. Her body shook with need and anticipation. *Mine*, she mused possessively, her eyes taking in every inch of him. *All mine. Forever.*

And then he was down, crouched like the cat he was, starting at her ankles, kissing his way. Karen gasped with each warm, wet press of his lips. The inside of her knees, up her thighs, then pausing for a moment to lap at her wet pussy. Instantly, she spread her legs. Giving him better access. A soft growl exited his throat as he licked her. Slow, drugging licks that sent fire roaring through her.

"Please," she begged, knowing that with just a few more laps to her sex, she was going come. "Please, Reaux. I want you inside of me."

He growled his response, but did as she asked, moving upward. Her belly, her ribs, her right nipple. Karen was losing her mind. She wrapped her legs around him, hooking her ankles against his hard backside and squeezing herself against his long, hard cock. Reaux groaned, cursed, then ground himself against her slick pussy.

It was as if she'd waited a lifetime for this, for him. He was the one. Her only one. Her love. Her life. Her family. And she was desperate to know what it felt like to have him inside her. So deep she was claimed.

With a growl of her own she reached between

their bodies, fisted his rock-hard cock and placed the head of it at her entrance.

On a wicked, black snarl, Reaux's head came up. Gray eyes flashed fire and need.

"Please," she begged. "Can't go slow. Not the first time."

He cupped her face then, gave her a dark, hungry smile, and as he slowly entered her, he lowered his head and kissed her. Slow, drugging, sensual. A groan vibrated in Karen's throat with each incredible inch. And when she was full, when he was so deep she felt unable to think or breathe—just feel—he started to move.

All around them was the bayou. Green and cool and full of life. And her male was making love to her. For the first time. She reached for him, gripped his tight ass and held on. Indy had been right. A Pantera male was something else entirely. A shocking and intense lover, a harsh predator, a valued friend, and a fierce ally.

And family.

"I love you, Reaux," she called out as he thrust into her, hard and deep and everlasting. And when he sent her over the edge, crying and begging for more, the sunshine cocooning them in its warmth, Karen knew she was well and truly claimed.

In heart.
In body.
In mind.
And in spirit.

EXCERPT: KILL WITHOUT MERCY (ARES SECURITY)
BY ALEXANDRA IVY

PROLOGUE

Few people truly understood the meaning of 'hell on earth.'

The five soldiers who had been held in the Taliban prison in southern Afghanistan, however, possessed an agonizingly intimate knowledge of the phrase.

There was nothing like five weeks of brutal torture to teach a man that there are worse things than death.

It should have broken them. Even the most hardened soldiers could shatter beneath the acute psychological and physical punishment. Instead the torment only honed their ruthless determination to escape their captors.

In the dark nights they pooled their individual resources.

KILL WITHOUT MERCY EXCERPT
ALEXANDRA IVY

Rafe Vargas, a covert ops specialist. Max Grayson, trained in forensics. Hauk Laurensen, a sniper who was an expert with weapons. Teagan Moore, a computer wizard. And Lucas St. Clair, the smooth-talking hostage negotiator.

Together they forged a bond that went beyond friendship. They were a family bound by the grim determination to survive.

KILL WITHOUT MERCY EXCERPT
ALEXANDRA IVY

CHAPTER ONE

Friday nights in Houston meant crowded bars, loud music and ice-cold beer. It was a tradition that Rafe and his friends had quickly adapted to suit their own tastes when they moved to Texas five months ago.

After all, none of them were into the dance scene. They were too old for half-naked coeds and casual hookups. And none of them wanted to have to scream over pounding music to have a decent conversation.

Instead, they'd found The Saloon, a small, cozy bar with lots of polished wood, a jazz band that played softly in the background, and a handful of locals who knew better than to bother the other customers. Oh, and the finest tequila in the city.

They even had their own table that was reserved for them every Friday night.

Tucked in a back corner, it was shrouded in shadows and well away from the long bar that ran the length of one wall. A perfect spot to observe without being observed.

And best of all, situated so no one could sneak up from behind.

It might have been almost two years since they'd returned from the war, but none of them had forgotten.

Lowering your guard, even for a second, could mean death.

Lesson. Fucking. Learned.

Tonight, however, it was only Rafe and Hauk at the table, both of them sipping tequila and eating peanuts from a small bucket.

Lucas was still in Washington D.C., working his contacts to help drum up business for their new security business, ARES. Max had remained at their new offices, putting the final touches on his precious forensics lab, and Teagan was on his way to the bar after installing a computer system that would give Homeland Security a hemorrhage if they knew what he was doing.

Leaning back in his chair, Rafe intended to spend the night relaxing after a long week of hassling with the red tape and bullshit regulations that went into opening a new business, when he made the mistake of checking his messages.

"Shit."

He tossed his cellphone on the polished surface of the wooden table, a tangled ball of emotions lodged in the pit of his stomach.

Across the table Hauk sipped his tequila and studied Rafe with a lift of his brows.

At a glance, the two men couldn't be more different.

Rafe had dark hair that had grown long enough to touch the collar of his white button-down shirt along with dark eyes that were lushly framed by long, black lashes. His skin remained tanned dark bronze despite the fact it was late September, and his body was honed with muscles that came from working on the small ranch he'd just purchased, not the gym.

Hauk, on the other hand, had inherited his Scandinavian father's pale blond hair that he kept cut short, and brilliant blue eyes that held a cunning intelligence. He had a narrow face with sculpted features that were usually set in a stern expression.

And it wasn't just their outward appearance that made them so different.

Rafe was hot tempered, passionate and willing to trust his gut instincts.

Hauk was aloof, calculating, and mind-numbingly anal. Not that Hauk would admit he was OCD. He preferred to call himself detail-oriented.

Which was exactly why he was a successful sniper. Rafe, on the other hand, had been trained in combat rescue. He was capable of making quick decisions, and ready to change strategies on the fly.

"Trouble?" Hauk demanded.

Rafe grimaced. "The real estate agent left a message saying she has a buyer for my grandfather's house."

Hauk looked predictably confused. Rafe had been bitching about the need to get rid of his grandfather's house since the old man's death a year ago.

"Shouldn't that be good news?"

"It would be if I didn't have to travel to Newton to clean it out," Rafe said.

"Aren't there people you can hire to pack up the shit and send it to you?"

"Not in the middle of fucking nowhere."

Hauk's lips twisted into a humorless smile. "I've been in the middle of fucking nowhere, amigo, and it ain't Kansas," he said, the shadows from the past darkening his eyes.

"Newton's in Iowa, but I get your point," Rafe conceded. He did his best to keep the memories in the past where they belonged. Most of the time he was successful. Other times the demons refused to be leashed. "Okay, it's not the hell hole we crawled out of, but the town might as well be living in another century. I'll have to go deal with my grandfather's belongings myself."

Hauk reached to pour himself another shot of tequila from the bottle that had been waiting for them in the center of the table.

Like Rafe, he was dressed in an Oxford shirt, although his was blue instead of white, and he was wearing black dress pants instead of jeans.

"I know you think it's a pain, but it's probably for the best."

Rafe glared at his friend. The last thing he wanted was to drive a thousand miles to pack up the belongings of a cantankerous old man who'd never forgiven Rafe's father for walking away from Iowa. "Already trying to get rid of me?"

"Hell no. Of the five of us, you're the..."

"I'm afraid to ask," Rafe muttered as Hauk hesitated.

"The glue," he at last said.

Rafe gave a bark of laughter. He'd been called a lot of things over the years. Most of them unrepeatable. But glue was a new one. "What the hell does that mean?"

Hauk settled back in his seat. "Lucas is the smooth-talker, Max is the heart, Teagan is the brains and I'm the organizer." The older man shrugged.

"You're the one who holds us all together. ARES would never have happened without you."

Rafe couldn't argue. After returning to the States, the five of them had been transferred to separate hospitals to treat their numerous injuries. It would have been easy to drift apart. The natural instinct was to avoid anything that could remind them of the horror they'd endured.

But Rafe had quickly discovered that returning to civilian life wasn't a simple matter of buying a home and getting a 9-to-5 job.

He couldn't bear the thought of being trapped in a small cubicle eight hours a day, or returning to an empty condo that would never be a home.

It felt way too much like the prison he'd barely escaped.

Besides, he found himself actually missing the bastards.

Who else could understand his frustrations? His inability to relate to the tedious, everyday problems of civilians? His lingering nightmares?

So giving into his impulse, he'd phoned Lucas, knowing he'd need the man's deep pockets to finance his crazy scheme. Astonishingly, Lucas hadn't even hesitated before saying 'yes.' It'd been the same for Hauk and Max and Teagan.

All of them had been searching for something that would not only use their considerable skills, but would make them feel as if they hadn't been put out to pasture like bulls that were past their prime.

And that was how ARES had been born.

Now he frowned at the mere idea of abandoning

his friends when they were on the cusp of realizing their dream.

"Then why are you encouraging me to leave town when we're just getting ready to open for business?"

"Because he was your family."

"Bull. Shit." Rafe growled. "The jackass turned his back on my father when he joined the army. "He never did a damned thing for us."

"And that's why you need to go," Hauk insisted. "You need—"

"You say the word closure and I'll put my fist down your throat," Rafe interrupted, grabbing his glass and tossing back the shot of tequila.

Hauk ignored the threat with his usual arrogance. "Call it what you want, but until you forgive the old man for hurting your father it's going to stay a burr in your ass."

Rafe shrugged. "It matches my other burrs."

Without warning, Hauk leaned forward, his expression somber. "Rafe, it's going to take a couple of weeks before we're up and running. Finish your business and come back when you're ready."

Rafe narrowed his gaze. There was no surprise that Hauk was pressing him to deal with his past. Deep in his heart, Rafe knew his friend was right.

But he could hear the edge in Hauk's voice that made him suspect this was more than just a desire to see Rafe dealing with his resentment toward his grandfather. "There's something you're not telling me."

"Hell, I have a thousand things I don't tell you," Hauk mocked, lifting his glass with a mocking smile. "I am a vast, boundless reservoir of knowledge."

A classic deflection. Rafe laid his palms on the table, leaning forward. "You're also full of shit." His voice was hard with warning. "Now spill."

"Pushy bastard." Hauk's smile disappeared. "Fine. There was another note left on my desk."

Rafe hissed in frustration.

The first note had appeared just days after they'd first arrived in Houston.

It'd been left in Hauk's car with a vague warning that he was being watched.

They'd dismissed it as a prank. Then a month later a second note had been taped to the front door of the office building they'd just rented.

This one had said the clock was ticking.

Once again Hauk had tried to pretend it was nothing, but Teagan had instantly installed a state of the art alarm system, while Lucas had used his charm to make personal friends among the local authorities and encouraged them to keep a close eye on the building.

"What the fuck?" Rafe clenched his teeth as a chill inched down his spine. He had a really, really bad feeling about the notes. "Did you check the security footage?"

"Well gosh, darn," Hauk drawled. "Why didn't I think of that?"

"No need to be a smartass."

Hauk drained his glass of tequila. "But I'm so good at it."

"No shit."

Hauk pushed aside his empty glass and met Rafe's worried gaze.

KILL WITHOUT MERCY EXCERPT
ALEXANDRA IVY

"Look, everything that can be done is being done. Teagan has tapped into the traffic cameras. Unless our visitor is a ghost he'll eventually be spotted arriving or leaving. Max is working his forensic magic on the note, and Lucas has asked the local cops to contact the neighboring businesses to see if they've noticed anything unusual."

"I don't like this, Hauk."

"It's probably some whackadoodle I've pissed off," the older man assured him. "Not everyone finds me as charming as you do."

Rafe gave a short, humorless laugh. Hauk was intelligent, fiercely loyal, and a natural leader. He could also be cold, arrogant, and inclined to assume he was always right. "Hard to believe."

"I know, right?" Hauk batted his lashes. "I'm a doll."

"You're a pain in the ass, but no one gets to threaten you but me," Rafe said. "These notes feel... off."

Hauk reached to pour himself another shot, his features hardening into an expression that warned he was done with the discussion.

"We've got it covered, Rafe. Go to Kansas."

"Iowa."

"Wherever." Hauk grabbed the cellphone on the table and pressed it into Rafe's hand. "Take care of the house."

Rafe reluctantly rose to his feet. He could argue until he was blue in the face, but Hauk would deal with the threat in his own way.

"Call if you need me."

"Yes, mother."

With a roll of his eyes, Rafe made his way through the crowd that filled the bar, ignoring the inviting glances from the women who deliberately stepped into his path.

He was man enough to fully appreciate what was on offer. But since his return stateside he'd discovered the promise of a fleeting hookup left him cold.

He didn't know what he wanted, but he hadn't found it yet.

He'd just reached the door when he met Teagan entering the bar.

The large, heavily muscled man with dark caramel skin, golden eyes and his hair shaved close to his skull didn't look like a computer wizard. Hell, he looked like he should be riding with the local motorcycle gang. And it wasn't just that his arms were covered with tattoos or that he was wearing fatigues and leather shit-kickers.

It was in the air of violence that surrounded him and his don't-screw-with-me expression.

Of course, he'd been thrown in jail at the age of thirteen for hacking into a bank to make his mother's car loan disappear. So he'd never been the traditional nerd.

"I'm headed out."

"So early?" Teagan glanced toward the crowd that was growing progressively louder. "The party's just getting started."

"I'll take a rain check." Rafe said. "I'm leaving town for a few days."

"Business?"

"Family."

"Fuck," Teagan muttered.

The man rarely discussed his past, but he'd never made a secret of the fact he deeply resented the father who'd beaten his mother nearly to death before abandoning both of them.

"Exactly," Rafe agreed before leaning forward to keep anyone from overhearing his words. "Keep an eye on Hauk. I don't think he's taking the threats seriously enough."

"Got a hunch?" Teagan demanded.

Rafe nodded, as always surprised at how easily his friends accepted his gut instincts. "If someone wanted to hurt him, they wouldn't send a warning," he pointed out. "Especially not when he's surrounded by friends who are experts in tracking down and destroying enemies."

Teagan nodded. "True."

"So either the bastard has a death-wish. Or he's playing a game of cat and mouse."

"What would be the point?"

Rafe didn't have a clue. But people didn't taunt a man as dangerous as Hauk unless they were prepared for the inevitable conclusion.

One of them would die.

Rafe gave a sharp shake of his head. "Let's hope we have culprit in custody when we find out. Otherwise..."

"Nothing's going to happen to him, my man." Teagan grabbed Rafe's shoulder. "Not on my watch."

ABOUT ALEXANDRA IVY

Alexandra Ivy is a *New York Times* and *USA Today* bestselling author of the Guardians of Eternity, as well as the Sentinels, Dragons of Eternity and ARES series. After majoring in theatre she decided she prefers to bring her characters to life on paper rather than stage. She lives in Missouri with her family. Visit her website at alexandraivy.com.

BOOK LIST

GUARDIANS OF ETERNITY

WHEN DARKNESS ENDS
ISBN: 978-1420125177

HUNT THE DARKNESS

WHEN DARKNESS COMES

ARES SERIES

KILL WITHOUT MERCY
ISBN: 978-1420137552

BAYOU HEAT SERIES

ICE/REAUX

RAGE/KILLION

BAYOU HEAT COLLECTION ONE
ISBN: 2940148435235
July 19, 2013

BAYOU HEAT COLLECTION TWO
ISBN: 2940149957668

ANGEL/HISS
ISBN: 9780986064173

MICHEL/STRIKER

DRAGONS OF ETERNITY

BURNED BY DARKNESS

SENTINELS:

BLOOD LUST
May 31, 2016
978-1420137590

ON THE HUNT

ABOUT LAURA WRIGHT

New York Times and USA Today Bestselling Author, Laura Wright is passionate about romantic fiction. Though she has spent most of her life immersed in acting, singing and competitive ballroom dancing, when she found the world of writing and books and endless cups of coffee she knew she was home. Laura is the author of the bestselling Mark of the Vampire series and the USA Today bestselling series, Bayou Heat, which she co-authors with Alexandra Ivy.

Laura lives in Los Angeles with her husband, two young children and three loveable dogs.

BOOK LIST

Mark of the Vampire
Book 1: Eternal Hunger
978-0451231499

Book 2: Eternal Kiss
978-0451233844

Book 2.5: Eternal Blood (Especial)

Book 3: Eternal Captive
978-0451235879

Book 4: Eternal Beast
978-0451237729

Book 4.5: Eternal Beauty (Especial)

Book 5: Eternal Demon
978-0451239754

Book 6: Eternal Sin (November 5, 2013)
978-0451240163

Bayou Heat Series

Bayou Heat Raphael & Parish
Book #1 and #2 in the Bayou Heat Series
ISBN 978-0-9886245-0-4

Bayou Heat Bayon & Jean-Baptiste
Book #3 and #4 in the Bayou Heat Series

Bayou Heat Talon & Xavier
Book #5 and #6 in the Bayou Heat Series

Bayou Heat Sebastian & Aristide
Book #7 and #8 in the Bayou Heat Series

Bayou Heat Lian & Roch
Book #9 and #10 in the Bayou Heat Series

Bayou Heat Hakan & Severin
Book #11 and #12 in the Bayou Heat Series

Bayou Heat Angel & Hiss
Book #13 and #14 in the Bayou Heat Series

Bayou Heat Michel & Striker
Book #15 and #16 in the Bayou Heat Series

Bayou Heat Rage & Killian
Book #17 and #18 in the Bayou Heat Series
1001 Dark Nights Novella

Bayou Heat Ice & Reaux
Book #19 and #20 in the Bayou Heat Series
January 7, 2016

WICKED INK CHRONICLES
(New Adult Series- 17+)

FIRST INK
Book 1 in the WICKED INK CHRONICLES

SHATTERED INK
Book 2 in the WICKED INK CHRONICLES series

REBEL INK
Book 3 in the WICKED INK CHRONICLES

CAVANAUGH BROTHERS
BRANDED
Book 1 in THE CAVANAUGH BROTHERS series

BROKEN
Book 2 in THE CAVANAUGH BROTHERS series

BRASH
Book 3 in THE CAVANAUGH BROTHERS series

BONDED
Book 4 in THE CAVANAUGH BROTHERS series

MASTERS OF SEDUCTION SERIES VOLUME ONE

MASTERS OF SEDUCTION SERIES VOLUME TWO

INCUBUS TALES

SPURS, STRIPES and SNOW Series

SINFUL IN SPURS
Book 1 in the SPURS, STRIPES and SNOW Series

CPSIA information can be obtained
at www.ICGtesting.com
Printed in the USA
LVHW091027020222
710052LV00003B/62